LOVE INSPIRED

INSPIRATIONAL ROMANCE

The Amish Newcomer

PATRICE LEWIS

Can an *Englisch*
city girl ever
become one of
the Plain People?

LOVE INSPIRED
INSPIRATIONAL ROMANCE

Uplifting stories of faith, forgiveness and hope.

Fall in love with stories where faith helps guide you through life's challenges, and discover the promise of a new beginning.

AVAILABLE THIS MONTH

SEEKING REFUGE
LENORA WORTH

A HOME FOR HER DAUGHTER
JILL WEATHERHOLT

THE AMISH NEWCOMER
PATRICE LEWIS

WITH ALL HER HEART
KAT BROOKES

HIS TRUE PURPOSE
DANICA FAVORITE

A LOVE REDEEMED
LISA JORDAN

ISBN-13: 978-1-335-48836-7
9 781335 488367
50599

EAN

LIATMIFC0920

"Since I'm here for so long, I wanted to fit in...

"...But I'm hoping everyone can forgive me for any blunders I make."

"Oh, they will." Isaac fell silent as Leah padded along. "Will you be attending the hot dog roast at the Millers' tonight?"

"I'm not sure it's polite to show up without an invitation."

"The Millers won't mind. They'll have a large crowd of *youngies* anyway, so one extra person won't matter."

"What's a hot dog roast?"

"Just as it sounds. They have a long pit where they build a fire, so everyone has a chance to stand by the flames and cook their hot dogs."

"But what do they do, besides eat hot dogs?"

"Talk. Sing. Play games. And sometimes flirt." He grinned at her.

Leah caught her breath. If she didn't know any better, she might have thought Isaac was flirting with *her*. If so, it was subtle almost to the point of invisibility.

And there was no possible way she could flirt back...not with a man bound within the rules of a faith she didn't share.

Living on a remote self-sufficient homestead in North Idaho, **Patrice Lewis** is a Christian wife, mother, author, blogger, columnist and speaker. She has practiced and written about rural subjects for almost thirty years. When she isn't writing, Patrice enjoys self-sufficiency projects, such as animal husbandry, small-scale dairy production, gardening, food preservation and canning, and homeschooling. She and her husband have been married since 1990 and have two daughters.

Books by Patrice Lewis

Love Inspired

The Amish Newcomer

Visit the Author Profile page at Harlequin.com.

The Amish Newcomer

Patrice Lewis

LOVE INSPIRED
INSPIRATIONAL ROMANCE

LOVE INSPIRED®
INSPIRATIONAL ROMANCE

ISBN-13: 978-1-335-48836-7

The Amish Newcomer

Copyright © 2020 by Patrice Lewis

Recycling programs
for this product may
not exist in your area.

This edition published by arrangement with Harlequin Books S.A.

For questions and comments about the quality of this book, please contact us at CustomerService@Harlequin.com.

Love Inspired
22 Adelaide St. West, 40th Floor
Toronto, Ontario M5H 4E3, Canada
www.Harlequin.com

Printed in U.S.A.

And that ye study to be quiet, and to do your own business, and to work with your own hands, as we commanded you; That ye may walk honestly toward them that are without, and that ye may have lack of nothing.
—*1 Thessalonians* 4:11–12

To God, for His many gifts.

To my husband and two daughters,
my biggest blessings.

To my agent, for his encouragement.

To Patty and Wendy,
for their decades of love and support.

To Cheryl,
for her mentoring.

Thank you all.

Chapter One

Leah Porte clutched her suitcase and climbed out of the dusty Subaru in front of a white farmhouse several miles outside the tiny hamlet of Pikeville, Ohio. The moment she closed the car door, the driver sped off in a cloud of dust and disappeared over a low hill, taking with it her last link to anything familiar.

Silence reigned.

Rustling cornfields bordered the large house on two sides. One by one, children gathered on the wide front porch and stared at her. Six children in all, three boys and three girls. She expected them to pepper her with questions, but they were silent, watching her with large blue eyes.

She put her suitcase down, wondering how odd she looked in her beige slacks and print blouse. The children were dressed more or less the same, the boys in black trousers and black suspenders, the girls in plain dresses with white bonnets of some sort. Only their bold colors on shirts or dresses—dark blue, green, purple, burgundy, pale blue—distinguished one child's garments from another's.

The middle daughter caught her eye. At first Leah thought she was a young child, but the mature features quickly confirmed she was just short, a little person, in fact. The young woman nodded and gave her a hint of a smile, her own eyes lingering on the angry red scar on Leah's right cheek.

"Well." Edith, the children's mother, spoke into the lengthening silence. Large with pregnancy, she appeared comfortable in her white *kapp* and loose blue dress. "The first thing to do with you is get you out of your *Englischer* clothes and into something Plain. The sooner you look Amish, the faster you'll fit in." Leah heard the cadence of a second language in the older woman's voice.

"I—I can't thank you enough for taking me in." Leah fiddled with a button on her blouse. "I've never been in a witness protection program before. This whole experience has been bewildering."

"You'll have time to tell us about it later." Edith tugged her apron straight. "But for now let's get you dressed. Amos, please carry her suitcase upstairs."

One of the middle children, a boy around ten, snagged her suitcase and went clattering into the house. Edith followed, gesturing to Leah.

As expected, the home was simple and sparsely furnished, but airy and bright. Leah followed Edith up a narrow flight of stairs with no pictures on the walls and no adornment besides the banister.

"We have two guest rooms." Edith puffed a little as she climbed the stairs. "I'm certain sure we'll be filling them with *kinner* soon enough. My next *boppli* is due in almost three months, but for now you'll have the room to yourself."

A corridor ran the length of the upstairs, with numerous open doors on either side. The young boy turned in to a doorway, dropped the suitcase and stepped out of the room. Edith led the way in and Leah followed.

The colorful quilt, glowing in a patch of sunlight, caught her eye. Beyond that, the room was plain to the point of austere, with a serviceable pine dresser, a bedside table with a kerosene lamp, and a comfortable-looking rocking chair. The only wall adornment was a pine board with hooks that a variety of garments hung from.

"Since we weren't sure what size you were, we borrowed a couple dresses from my *schweschder* as well as my oldest *dochder.*" Edith turned and looked Leah over. "My Sarah is about your height, so we'll start with her dress." Removing a forest-green garment from the hook, Edith held it in front of Leah. "*Ja*, I think this will fit."

Leah sat down in the rocking chair and started unlacing her shoes. "Here," Edith said, placing the dress on the bed. "You'll see the back is done up with snaps. Some sects only use hooks and eyes, but our community's *Ordnung* is less strict."

Leah almost laughed. "It sounds like you've explained Amish dress to outsiders before."

Edith shrugged. "Tourists ask sometimes."

"Have you ever taken in anyone from witness protection?"

"*Nee*, not us. But others in our community, *ja*. We prefer not to get involved in criminal activities. But once in a while we are asked, especially since our bishop has non-Amish relatives in law enforcement. Each time, he has to decide whether the case is serious enough for us to involve ourselves. In your situation, he felt it would not disrupt our community and it would provide you with the protection you need."

"And I won't corrupt your children." Leah attempted some humor. "I promise not to tell your daughters about the latest trends in fashion and makeup."

"Danke." Edith handed her the dress. "Try this on. I'll wait in the hall to do up your snaps when you're ready." She smiled and slipped out the door.

Leah stepped into the cotton garment. The back and waist gapped as she scooped her clothes off the floor, somehow compelled to be tidy in this strange home. Then she walked to the door and cracked it open. "Ready."

Edith stepped into the room and closed the door behind her. *"Gut,* it looks like it fits." She spun Leah around and did up the snaps.

"Will I always need help getting dressed?"

"Oh, you'll get the hang of it in no time. But if you need help, my two oldest *dochder* are in the bedroom just across the hall."

The dress was not formfitting but blousy. "Next, the apron." Edith removed a gray garment from a hook and slipped it over Leah's arms. "It pins this way. Now the *kapp.*"

The starched head covering looked to be made of organza. "Let's do your hair first." Edith studied Leah. "What a blessing it's not short."

Leah tucked a strand behind her ears. "What do I have to do?"

"Twist it into a ponytail, then I'll help you pin it up."

It took a few minutes to get the ponytail to Edith's satisfaction. With quick gestures she twisted and wound Leah's hair into a bun and tucked in bobby pins. "The *kapp* goes on like this."

"Why do Amish women wear these?" Leah touched the lightweight covering.

"The Bible tells us to keep our heads covered. We always wear prayer *kapps*, so if we need to pray during the day, our heads are covered and sacred to *Gott*."

Leah wondered if such trappings were necessary, but Edith obviously believed what she said, and Leah was in no position to naysay anything. As an agnostic staying with believers—and as a modern career woman staying with the Amish—Leah knew when to remain quiet.

"I feel like a hypocrite," she murmured, after Edith stepped back and examined her.

"Why?"

"Because I'm not Amish. Somehow wearing this *kapp* feels…well, holy."

Edith chuckled. "None of us are holy. We're just ordinary. Plain. Sometimes I think it's the *Englisch* who make more of Amish *kapps* than we do. Oh, one last thing. Take out your earrings. Plain women wear no jewelry."

Leah had worn the simplest earrings she owned, a pair of small gold studs. Apparently even that was too much. With a sigh she removed the jewelry and laid them on the dresser.

Edith stepped back and looked her over, then nodded. "You'll do."

"But people will know I'm not Amish." Leah clasped

her hands. "I haven't spoken a word of German since my college days, and I'm totally unfamiliar with your culture."

"No one expects you to be Amish. We've told no one you're in witness protection, merely that you're someone recovering from a bad car accident. That will explain the scar. The fewer who know why you're here, the better. Our *kinner* won't say anything. All you need to do is to keep your mouth shut as much as possible and don't talk to any *Englisch*." The older woman paused. "How much *Deitsch* do you speak?"

"*Gerade genug, um mich selbst in Verlegenheit zu bringen.* Just enough to embarrass myself." Leah gave a faint smile.

"Ah, High German. You'll find we speak our own dialect of *Deitsch*. It's quite different, though you might be able to follow some of the Sabbath meetings. Now let's go downstairs and I'll introduce you to the *familye*. It's almost dinnertime anyway."

Leah knew enough to recognize that the word "dinner" actually meant lunch, and "supper" meant dinner. Her stomach growled. "What about shoes?"

Edith glanced down at Leah's bare feet. "Most unmarried women go barefoot in warmer weather."

Leah winced. "I'll warn you—I have very tender feet. I'm not used to going without shoes."

"They'll toughen up quick enough. *Komm* now." Edith led the way out of the bedroom.

Leah padded behind, down the stairs, through the living room and into a spacious kitchen with an enormous wood cookstove. The two older daughters stirred pots on the stove. The younger girl set plain white plates on the table.

"*Kinner*, this is Leah Porte. Leah, these are my *dochder*."

The girls nodded acknowledgment. Leah tried not to feel self-conscious about the obvious red scar on her face when she noticed lingering glances, but no one mentioned it.

"My *mann* and *söhne* should be here in a few minutes." Edith picked up a spoon and stirred a boiling pot. "Leah, why don't you slice some bread? That will give you something to do."

The oldest daughter reached for some items and handed Leah a wooden cutting board and bread knife. "You can set up here." She pointed to a bare spot at the kitchen counter. "This is the loaf to cut up."

The baguette-shaped bread was still warm. "Thank you." Leah ducked her head and sliced the bread. She stacked the half-inch slices to one side.

"*Mamm*, where will Leah sit?" The youngest daughter paused with plates in her hands.

"Over there, between the older girls."

A clatter of footsteps on the porch heralded the boys, who headed to the sink to wash their hands without being told.

"Ah, is this our new visitor?" exclaimed a hearty voice.

Leah turned. A tall, burly man with the requisite Amish beard, black suspenders, and a twinkle in his eyes walked into the kitchen. She wiped her right hand on her apron and held it out. "How do you do? I'm Leah Porte."

"*Gut* to meet you. I'm Ivan Byler. *Welkom*." He gave her hand one hard pump. "Have you met our *kinner*?"

"Just the girls. Though Amos carried my suitcase upstairs." Leah smiled at the boy.

Ivan rattled off the names of his sons, who one by one stepped forward to shake her hand.

"You have beautiful children," concluded Leah. "Will you be having a boy or girl next?"

"We won't know until it's born. It's entirely up to the Lord." Edith rubbed her stomach and smiled. "Where's Isaac?" she added to her husband.

"He's coming soon. He's just finishing up one last thing."

"Isaac? Another son?" inquired Leah.

"*Nee.* Isaac is a friend. He's working with me in the shop for a few weeks to earn a bit of extra money."

"I understand you make furniture." Leah directed her question at Ivan. "What kind?"

"Whatever is needed." The man moved to the sink, pumped the handle and washed his hands. "I get special orders, but I also have some pieces in stores. Beds, dressers, tables, rocking chairs, bookshelves. I like working with wood."

Leah detected a combination of humility and satisfaction in the man's voice. Before coming to Ohio, she had learned pride was a grievous sin among the Amish. Obviously she wasn't going to get Ivan to brag about his accomplishments, which made her think he was a very skilled craftsman indeed.

The children seated themselves, and the older girls carried platters and bowls to the table.

"Here comes Isaac." Edith nodded toward the driveway. "Why does he have his camera? I thought he was finished taking pictures of the shop."

"He said he wanted just a couple more." Ivan helped his youngest son into a chair.

"Pictures? With a camera?" Leah raised her eyebrows. "I thought you didn't use cameras."

"*Ja*, well, Isaac is…is different." Edith jerked her head toward the screen door, where the man could be seen, then added in a whisper, "I'll explain later."

Through the screen door, she saw a man whose bright blue shirt matched his eyes. Unlike Ivan, he wore no beard, though he had the same curly brown hair and straw hat.

"*Welkom*, Isaac!" called Edith.

Isaac Sommer heard the invitation through the screen door. He stepped inside. *"Danke."*

"Isaac, we have a visitor. This is Leah Porte. She's an *Englischer* friend of ours, staying with us a few months. Leah, this is Isaac Sommer."

For a moment Isaac was struck dumb by the newcomer. With her dark hair tamed back under a *kapp*, and her chocolate eyes, he barely noticed the ugly red scar bisecting her right cheek in light of the newcomer's stunning beauty.

He swallowed as Leah stepped forward and held out her hand. "How do you do?"

He wiped his hand on his trousers. "Fine, *danke*. Where do you come from?"

"California."

"That's far away."

"Yes." She glanced at the floor. "Not far enough," she murmured.

"Please, sit. Both of you." Edith gestured toward the table.

Isaac found himself opposite Leah and gazed at her as the family gathered around the table. When all heads bowed in silence, he found himself praying he could get to know the visitor better.

At once chatter broke out as the family reached for food. Isaac's appetite fled. He tried not to stare.

"We hope you'll have a pleasant stay with us." Ivan scooped corn onto his plate and added a dollop of butter.

"I—I'm not familiar with your day-to-day activities." The woman toyed with her fork. "I don't want to be seen as a freeloader, but I don't know if I can pull my weight."

"Freeloader?" repeated Edith.

"Schmarotzer," translated Ivan. "What is it you did before you came here?"

"I was a television journalist. I reported news stories from the street and in front of a camera," she replied. Isaac saw her touch her wounded cheek and glance toward him. "But after my…my car accident, I couldn't do my job anymore."

Journalist! What kind of God-sent coincidence was that? He tamped down his excitement and smiled. "Maybe I should have you write some articles for my magazine."

"Magazine?"

"Yes, I publish a magazine." He pointed at the camera on the table.

"I was told the Amish didn't use cameras."

"*Ja*, well…" It was still a sensitive subject. He looked at his plate.

Into the short silence, Edith explained, "Isaac started a magazine for Plain People. He uses a computer to create it. The bishop gave him permission to use it."

"An Amish man using a computer? But I was told…"

"Many *Englischers* have misconceptions of how much technology the Leit allows," Ivan intervened. "You won't find computers in our homes, or those cell phones so many *Englischer* people carry. But while we try to live not *of* the world, we still live *in* the world, and sometimes technology is needed to keep our businesses running. It does no good if we can't compete among the *Englisch* and we lose our farms and our livelihood. So, some bishops have decided a little technology is allowed, as long as it doesn't affect the…the…" Ivan groped for a word. "The *zusammenhalt*…the *cohesion*, that's it…of our community."

"And it *hasn't*." Isaac hoped he didn't sound too defensive. He toyed with a glass of water.

"No, it hasn't," assured Edith.

"What's the magazine about?" Leah buttered a biscuit.

"Whatever appeals to Plain People. Farming. Businesses. Animal husbandry. Land management."

"And you want *me* to write for it?" she asked. He heard the twinge of sarcasm in her voice. "I don't know anything about those topics."

"But that's what a journalist does, ain't so? Learn about new topics," he replied. Her subtle opposition just made him more determined to entice her. "Besides, you're about to get a crash course in those topics while you stay here. Maybe you'll learn something."

"I already said I had no intention of being a free-loader."

He nodded. "*Gut.* Then prove it. You can write me an article about what you learn."

"Sure," she snapped. "How hard could it be?"

He grinned. "You'll find out soon enough."

"Now, now." Edith scooped some potatoes onto her youngest son's plate. "We'll keep you busy enough. Since it's late June, most of the heavy spring work is done as far as planting, but there's always gardening to do, and cooking, and laundry and other chores. Since you're *Englisch*, you haven't learned to do these things without electricity, so we'll teach you. And depending on how long you're here, when harvest comes we'll be canning and preserving. And then there's this little one…" She patted her stomach. "It's due in mid-September, so an extra pair of hands in the *haus* will be *welkom.*"

"And it will keep me here at the house." Leah ducked her head. "I'm not eager to be seen."

"Why not?" blurted Ivan, caught off-guard. "Oh, that? No one cares how you look. We see *Gott*'s love in everyone, regardless." He reached over and playfully chucked Rachel, his small adult daughter, under the chin. The young woman looked at her plate, but Isaac saw the pleased smile on her face.

"Where is the magazine sold?" Leah asked.

"All over our area," he replied. "Among both Amish and Mennonites who run stores, you'll find copies for sale."

Edith added, "He also mails it to people who live

farther away. He said the farthest away he's mailed one is Australia." She paused and seemed to marvel at the thought. "And he wants to photograph our workshop, to show what kind of furniture Ivan makes."

"So this is all new to you, then?" Isaac asked Leah.

She met his eyes. "Yes."

"Farm life in general, or Amish life?"

"Both."

"Then your insights actually would be very interesting in the magazine. A lot of people talk about the so-called simple life, but when they try it, they find it's not so simple."

"I'm not really into the simple-life stuff." She toyed with her fork. "I'm a modern woman, a career woman. I'm just here until I can get back on my feet and return to my profession." She looked over at Edith. "Is that how people think about the Amish, that they're all about simple living?"

"Yes," groaned Edith. "You'd be surprised."

"We don't live a simple life—we live a life devoted to *Gott*." Isaac took a bite of corn, swallowed and continued. "We think we can best do that by withdrawing from the world and doing things in a simpler way."

"Except when it comes to using a computer to run a magazine."

Isaac tried not to chuckle. He liked her feistiness. "Spitfire, eh?"

"So I've been told."

"Well, I look forward to seeing you put your money where your mouth is. You're in for a steep learning curve."

Leah sighed. "I know." She rubbed her eyes as if rubbing away false pride. "It's just that…well, I'm coming to realize my expensive college education and experience in the news industry hardly count anymore. All those years of schooling and work, wasted."

"Nothing is ever wasted," he assured her. "All you have to do is figure out how to apply what you have to your new life. *Gott* will provide."

He thought he saw a flash of anger in her eyes, but perhaps he was mistaken. The woman turned to Ivan and asked, "What do you farm?" in an obvious change of subject.

"Corn, a little wheat, and we have an apple orchard." Ivan replied. "The corn we sell. The apples we sell. The wheat we keep, along with the fruit from the rest of the orchard trees we grow. Most of our income is from my workshop." He looked at Isaac. "I have just a few more tasks for you this afternoon. It won't take long."

"*Ja*, sure, I can get back home then."

"May I see your workshop?" Leah asked Ivan.

"*Ja*, sure. After dinner, if you like."

"We're about finished anyway." Edith lifted her littlest son, who was wiggling, off his booster seat. She looked frazzled. "Someone needs to show Leah around the farm, but I also want you girls—" she addressed her daughters "—to bring some food to the Yoders. They're having a work party shortly to build a barn extension…"

"Why don't *I* show Leah around the farm?" offered Isaac. "After I finish up in the shop."

Edith lifted her eyebrows. "*Ja*, that would be helpful. *Danke*, Isaac."

But fascinating or not, he had to remember the yawning chasm between Leah Porte and himself. It was a chasm that could not be bridged.

Chapter Two

After dinner, Leah found herself washing dishes with the Byler daughters. "We're glad you're here," said Sarah, the oldest, whose dark blond hair and china-blue eyes made her look like a wholesome fashion model.

"Yes, we are," echoed Rachel, the short middle daughter. "Here, you can wipe." She handed Leah a dish towel.

Eliza, the youngest daughter, clattered around gathering dishes from the table and depositing them near the sink.

"How long will you be here?" Sarah asked, as she plunged her hands into soapy water.

"I don't know. They seem to think it will be months. I—I know I can't stay here forever, and I can't return to my former job, so I'm at something of a loss."

"*Gott* will provide." Rachel rinsed a plate and handed it to Leah.

Leah thinned her lips. Isaac had said the same thing. But God hadn't provided so well when it came to allowing her to use her education and skills to further her career. What did this Amish girl know of what it took to claw one's way to the top of one's profession in the dog-eat-dog world of television journalism?

She bit back the unwarranted retort. *It's not Rachel's fault my future is uncertain.* She owed this family a debt of gratitude and had no intention of taking out her change of circumstance on the innocent children.

Sarah chattered on. "And don't forget. Tonight we have a gathering at the Millers'." Her face lit up. "Hot dog roast!"

Rachel chuckled. "Light-minded," she told her sister, who stuck out her tongue before resuming her scrubbing.

"Are you both finished with school?" Leah set aside the wiped dishes.

"Oh yes. Years ago. We've both had our *rumspringa* too." Rachel rinsed cups.

"And perhaps things will change this November." Sarah's eyes twinkled. "You'll meet Aaron tonight." A rosy blush suffused the girl's cheeks.

"How old are you both?"

"Twenty," said Sarah.

"Eighteen," said Rachel. "How old are you?"

"Twenty-eight."

Sarah's brows rose. "And you're not married?"

"No. I was always too busy with my career to think about getting married."

Leah caught a surprised glance between the sisters. "Sad," murmured Rachel, her head ducked over the dishes.

In the English world, marriage was not the be-all and end-all of a woman's life, unlike in the Amish world.

"There." Sarah scrubbed the last pot and handed it to Rachel. "Eliza already wiped down the table and counters, so we can take the food to the Yoders. First we'll bring you to *Daed*'s shop so Isaac can give you the tour around the farm."

Rachel rinsed the pot and handed it to Leah, then wiped her own hands. Leah finished drying the pot, the girls put all the dishes away and she trailed after them as they headed for the front door.

A barnlike structure about thirty feet square stood on the other side of the gravel driveway, shaded by two fine maple trees. Tender in her bare feet, Leah had to walk slowly. June sunshine poured in through the large open rolling doors.

"Ah, here for the tour?" Ivan swept sawdust into a pile.

"Yes, please." Leah glanced around at the large space, which smelled of fresh wood shavings and was filled with tools she didn't recognize.

"We're going to the Yoders'," said Sarah. "We'll be back in an hour or so."

Ivan placed the broom in a corner and dusted off his hands. The young sons of the family were occupied with some task near the doorway.

Isaac walked over from a far corner, capping his camera. "Show her around here first, why don't you," he suggested to Ivan. "Then I'll take her around the farm."

"Ja." He turned to Leah. "As you know, we don't use electricity, but nothing in our *Ordnung* prevents us from using hydraulic and pneumatic power run by diesel compressors. We feel these technologies don't violate our dedication to living according to the biblical

Word of *Gott*. So this is my band saw. You can see up here how this pulley system runs from the motor to…"

Leah tried to follow Ivan's explanations as he described with enthusiasm the myriad tools and their uses. She was far more impressed with what he made. Half-finished rocking chairs, dressers, bed frames and tables all exhibited stunning handcrafted quality. Fully finished pieces sat along the walls of the shop, some covered in sheets, others draped with clear plastic to keep the dust off. Ignorant as she was of the intricacies of construction, even she recognized the quality and the beauty of the woodwork.

"I can see you never use particle board." She ran her fingers along a beautiful piece of maple on a dresser and thought of her pressed-sawdust dresser in Los Angeles.

"Of course not." Ivan pointed to lumber leaning against a wall and stored up in the rafters. "Several of us here in Pikeville buy our wood from a dealer who specializes in sustainable sources. If you have generations of woodworkers, you need generations of forests to keep us going. We use hardwoods such as northern red oak, cherry, maple, quartersawn white oak, mahogany, hickory, beech and elm. We also use softwoods like pine and cedar. Our dealer works with plantations in Appalachia and places in Tennessee and Michigan that grow trees just for us."

Leah grew intrigued by an industry she'd never considered before. "How many crafters use these plantations?"

"There are four woodworkers in our community," replied Ivan. "Regionally, among other Amish communities, there are…what, Isaac, about eight more?"

"Nine, I believe."

"And another dozen or so scattered in other states. We all get our lumber from these sources that have grown wood for craftsmen for about a century."

"Wow," murmured Leah.

Ivan rested his hand on the wooden flywheel of a nearby saw. "I was lucky to inherit some of the tools from factories in Michigan that used to make furniture. They broke up the factories in the 1960s, and some of the Amish craftsmen went in and bought up much of the old machinery they once used. The machinery was distributed around various communities. My grandfather obtained several pieces, and they've been passed down to me. My boys will take over this shop someday, and the tradition will continue." He reached out and ruffled the hair of his two young sons. The boys shuffled their feet and smiled. "And these two are showing great promise in following me as craftsmen."

Ivan's simple pride in his inherited skills, and his humble pleasure at passing those skills on to his own sons, touched Leah. How often had she ever come across such a structure? There was more to the Amish way of life than outsiders knew or appreciated. Just for a moment, the journalist in her stepped out of the shell of self-pity she had cultivated since her near-deadly encounter with gang members on that cold Los Angeles night six months ago.

She looked up and locked eyes with Isaac. He gave her a half smile, as if he understood the feelings behind the moment. Her cheeks grew warm, and she turned away. "And no one objects to having such young children around power tools?" she asked Ivan, to cover her emotions.

Isaac snorted with laughter before he discreetly turned it into a cough.

"How else can *kinner* learn but to follow the example of their parents?" inquired Ivan in genuine bewilderment.

How indeed? It was obvious that by the time these young boys turned eighteen, they would already be familiar with every tool, every technique and every aspect of furniture construction and would be able to make a living with their skills. It wasn't such a bad way.

"I think it's smart," she concluded out loud.

"But having Isaac here is a big help, especially when I'm on deadline. My boys are too young to work with the power tools yet." He nodded toward Isaac. "Go ahead and show her around, then I'll have just a bit more work for you this afternoon."

Isaac touched his hat brim and turned to Leah. "Ready to see the farm?"

"Sure. But walk slowly—I'm not used to walking around with bare feet."

She followed him outside into the warm June sunshine. He stopped and pointed at the acreage around the farm. "That's the corn crop. It's not very tall at the moment, of course, since it's just the end of June. There's an old saying—'Knee-high by the Fourth of July.' The idea is if the corn is up to a man's knees by that point, the harvest is likely to be good, *Gott* willing."

"And the Bylers sell the corn?" Leah looked over the verdant field.

"*Ja*. They have about four acres." Isaac made a wide

gesture. "It's sweet corn, and they mostly sell it at farm stands and a few grocery stores in the region. Anything left over they will usually can for the winter."

"They can their own corn?"

"Of course. How else will they preserve it? Everyone cans."

Not in Los Angeles, they don't, she thought.

Isaac led the way toward another barn and stepped into the shady interior. "The Bylers don't have a lot of animals compared to some people in our community. Ivan makes his living with the wood shop, not a dairy."

"So what do they have?"

"Jersey cows, a few pigs and of course the horses."

One horse put his nose over the half door of his stall. Isaac stroked him. "Most Amish don't breed or train their own horses. A lot of our buggy horses are former race horses. Ivan is busy in the shop, so he leaves the buggy training to others."

"How many horses do they have?"

"Just six. Two for buggies, four for draft work."

"And this is one of the buggy animals?"

"*Ja.* The draft animals are much bigger, of course." Ivan peered through a door. "Looks like they're out in the pasture at the moment."

Leah reached out and touched the horse's nose, which was soft as velvet. The animal didn't seem to mind, so she stroked him. "He's beautiful. I've never touched a horse before."

She glanced up in time to see Isaac's jaw drop.

"Never touched a horse?" he echoed.

"Of course not. There aren't a lot of horses in urban Los Angeles."

"Have you ever been on a farm?"

"No, I haven't."

"Then for sure and certain you've got a lot to learn."

Leah patted the horse again, smelled the rich horsey smell and thought perhaps there might be some rewarding experiences now that she was in witness protection.

Isaac moved toward another part of the barn. "Here's where Ivan milks the cows." One fawn-colored animal with huge doe eyes rested in the shade of the pen near the wide-open door leading to the pasture. Her jaws moved rhythmically. "The other three animals are out to pasture. You can just see them out there. Three of the calves are steers, so they'll get butchered later in the year."

Leah quailed at the thought of eating something the Byler family had raised. Of course she knew where meat came from but had never thought of coming face-to-face with the source. "What do they do with the milk?"

"Same thing my mother does, I assume. Make butter and cheese, sometimes yogurt. Anything extra goes to the pigs."

"What pigs?"

"These pigs." Isaac walked toward another portion of the barn.

The pigpen was a series of heavily reinforced stalls with open doorways leading outside. Four huge porkers wallowed in the shade, and one more stood in the doorway and sniffed at them. "You can't really tell from here, but the Bylers have a whole acre paddock for the pigs." Isaac pointed out the door. "They do well when they're given a bit of room to roam."

Leah sniffed. "They don't smell too bad. I would have thought pigs were dirty."

"No, they're very clean animals. They use a corner for a latrine and keep the rest of their pens tidy."

"The fence doesn't look very tall, though." Leah peered through the barn door to the outside paddock.

"Pigs don't jump, so it doesn't have to be tall. It just has to be strong at the bottom, because they root."

"Do a lot of people raise pigs?"

"*Ja.* The Bylers raise and sell piglets. Anything extra is butchered once the weather is cold enough."

"Do they freeze the meat?"

"No. Most of us don't have a freezer, of course, since we don't have electricity. We wait until winter, when *Gott* freezes it for us," replied Isaac. "Our bishop gave permission to put freezers at a place in town and store meat there, but a lot of people don't use that option. Most people smoke the meat, or can it, and the rest gets frozen in winter and eaten before spring comes." Isaac grinned. "*Frischi wascht,* yum."

"What's that?"

"Fresh sausage."

She looked down at the large animal lounging against the pen wall. "I'll never look at bacon the same way again," she muttered.

Isaac chuckled. "You get used to it quick enough. Most of us raise our own animals for meat, so they're raised humanely. To use *Englisch* terms, it's very green and sustainable."

Leah smiled. "I try to live a sustainable zero-waste lifestyle. Not that it was easy in Los Angeles."

"Then you've come to the right place." Isaac smiled

in high wattage. "There are few places overall as sustainable as an Amish community."

"Hmm." The journalist in her sat up and took notice. She wondered how many English reporters had written about this aspect of the Amish lifestyle. For all she knew, it was widely covered and she just wasn't aware of it.

"Maybe that should be the first article you write for my magazine," continued Isaac.

"I'm not interested in writing for your magazine."

"Why not?"

"Because I'm not a journalist anymore. Besides, who'd be interested in this kind of stuff?" She waved her arm.

She saw Isaac's expression tighten. She might be a little ashamed of her bluntness, but she had no interest in being roped into using her professional talents to write for some amateur magazine.

"*Ja*, well, I'll show you the orchard." He turned away.

She followed him from the barns and around the back of the house. Smallish trees in neat rows dotted a grassy field. On the edges, she counted six stacks of white boxes.

"These are apples." Isaac pulled a low-hanging branch lower. "See the fruit? They're only an inch across right now. Tiny, but they'll grow."

"And there are..." Leah counted under her breath. "Six, seven, eight, nine...twenty-five trees of each variety. I think Ivan said these apples are the ones he sells commercially?"

"*Ja*. It's not such a large orchard that they can't handle the work themselves, during the harvest." Isaac rubbed his chin. "I know Rachel loves working the apples. She's said it's one of her favorite things to do."

"I wonder how old these trees are."

"I'm guessing about twenty-two years or so." Isaac patted a trunk. "Ivan said his *daed* planted them as a wedding present when he and Edith were married."

"What a lovely gift." Leah was touched by the practical legacy.

"Those are the beehives." Isaac pointed at the stacks of white boxes. "Sometimes they sell honey, but I think they keep most of it. And of course the bees help with the fruit trees. Over there is the home orchard, where they grow other fruit. They have enough to share around, trading surplus in the community for what they don't grow themselves."

"Community," she mused.

"*Ja*, sure." Isaac's expression made it seem obvious. "It's what makes life worthwhile."

It's what makes life worthwhile. Yet had she ever experienced anything like the warm familiarity the Byler family had with their neighbors? *No.* While the journalist in her was intrigued by the concept, the human side of her longed to experience it, as well.

"Over there—" Isaac pointed "—you can see their wheat field. I know it looks something like a lawn at the moment, but that's because it's hard red spring wheat and should be ready to harvest in August."

"I've never heard of anyone growing their own wheat before," said Leah. "What do they do with it?"

"Make flour," replied Isaac. "It's not hard to do." He walked toward a fenced area. "Over here is their kitchen garden."

"*Kitchen* garden?" gasped Leah. "It's huge!"

"Well, it has to feed eight people and get them through the winter." He unlatched a gate and went inside. "They do a nice job of keeping it weeded."

"What is growing here?"

"Do you really want to hear the list, or would you rather know what they *don't* grow?"

"Uh, sure. Don't grow, I guess."

Isaac started ticking his fingers. "They don't grow lemons. Or coffee. Or lentils. Or rice. Or tea. Cinnamon. Peanuts. That kind of stuff."

She stared. "Sounds almost as if they grow *all* their own food." She dropped onto a nearby crate. "I don't think I've ever met anyone this self-sufficient."

"It's just how most people live." Isaac shrugged. "Everyone else does pretty much the same thing. What's the matter?"

Leah closed her gaping mouth with a snap. "I'm just overwhelmed, I guess." She lifted her hands and let them drop.

Her reaction seemed to amuse him. He chuckled. "City girl?"

"Completely." She sagged. "I'm afraid I have an awful lot to learn."

"Are you up for the task?"

Leah looked up at the hint of challenge. "That sounds like a dare."

"Maybe it is. The amount of work tends to discourage a lot of people who aren't Amish."

She lifted her chin. "Anything they throw at me, I can handle it."

"Gut." His grin held an almost fiendish overtone. "I look forward to seeing that."

It almost sounded like Isaac tried to provoke her. Why?

Before she could analyze it further, he held out a hand to assist her off the crate. "I think a quick peek at the chickens and then the outdoor tour is done. Sarah and Rachel can show you around the *haus* later. So," he added as he released her hand and fell into step beside her, "you said you were from Los Angeles?"

"Yes."

"Big city. Why are you here in Pikeville?"

Leah froze inside. It was the one question she didn't want to be asked, but at least she had a predetermined story she could tell, one that mingled with just enough truth to be plausible. "I was in a car accident." She touched her cheek. "It messed me up pretty badly. I used to work as a television journalist, but you can't be in television with a face like this. I—I needed to get away. I have friends who know the Bylers, and they invited me to stay with them until I heal up."

Unlike some other men she'd encountered, Isaac didn't seem to be put off by the scar in the slightest. "And then what? What happens after your face heals?"

"I don't know." Her shoulders slumped, and for a moment she allowed despair, which was never very far away, to claim her. "I don't know. I suppose I'll have to change my career, and it's something I'm reluctant to do. I loved being a TV journalist."

"Why are you dressed in Amish clothes? It seems unusual for a visitor."

That was a question she hadn't anticipated. "Uh…

uh…since I'm here for so long, I wanted to fit in. I speak a little German, and Edith thought it best if I didn't stand out. But I'm hoping everyone can forgive me for any blunders I make."

"Oh, they will." He fell silent as she padded along, her bare feet still tender. "Will you be attending the hot dog roast at the Millers' tonight?"

"I don't know. I'm not sure it's polite to show up without an invitation."

"The Millers won't mind. They'll have a large crowd of *youngies* anyway, so one extra person won't matter."

"What's a hot dog roast?"

"Just as it sounds. They have a long pit where they build a fire, so everyone has a chance to stand by the flames and cook their hot dogs."

"But what do they do, besides eat hot dogs?"

"Talk. Sing. Play games. And sometimes flirt." He grinned at her.

Leah caught her breath. If she didn't know any better, she might have thought Isaac was flirting with *her*. If so, it was subtle almost to the point of imperceptible. And there was no possible way she could flirt back, not with a man bound within the rules of a faith she didn't share.

She looked away. "I'm much older than Sarah or Rachel. Is this a gathering just for young people?"

"How old are you?" he blurted, then made a gesture as if to snatch the words back. "Sorry, I hope that wasn't rude."

His expression was so comical she laughed. "It's no secret. I'm twenty-eight."

"Ain't so? Me too."

"And you're not married? That seems unusual, from what I know of the Amish."

"I had—" He hesitated. "I spent some time away. Many years, in fact. Now I'm back and I intend to stay, but many of the women in the community aren't encouraging when it comes to risking their future with me. I have too much *Englisch* in me, they say."

She couldn't help but chuckle. "I assume *Englisch* is the catchall phrase for anyone who isn't Amish."

"*Ja.* It's not meant as a pejorative, just a distinguisher for anyone who isn't Amish. Here's the chicken coop."

Leah looked at the various clucking fowl. A rooster crowed lustily from one corner. "What kind are they?"

He pointed. "Ameraucana, Barred Rock, a couple of Buff Orpingtons and some Black Australorps. These are egg birds. In that coop over there—" Isaac pointed to a nearby spacious enclosure "—they raise Jersey Giants for meat."

So many meat animals… It was something Leah had never thought about before.

Isaac grinned. "It's quick and humane. They don't feel a thing."

How did he know what she was thinking? "I'm sure it is." She swallowed. "It's just a novelty for me to be looking meat in the eye."

"*Gott* provides us with meat. We are grateful for it."

"You still showing her around?" said a voice from behind.

Leah turned. Sarah and Rachel walked up with empty baskets in their hands.

"We're just finished," replied Isaac.

"I see." Rachel lifted a single brow, and her eyes darted between Leah and Isaac.

Leah's cheeks grew hot. It was clear Rachel thought there was interest between her and Isaac, and she wanted to nip that idea in the bud. "Yes. Well. Thank you for the tour, Isaac. I'm probably keeping you from a lot of work, so don't let me stop you."

"*Ja*, I have some things to finish up in the shop."

"Are you going to the Millers' hot dog roast tonight, Isaac?" Sarah asked Isaac.

"*Ja*, sure, I was planning to."

"Save a seat for Aaron, then."

"I will." Amusement tinged Isaac's voice. "I'll see you then." He flicked the brim of his hat, turned and marched away.

"I'll bet he didn't plan on it earlier," murmured Rachel, turning toward the house.

"Plan on what?" asked Leah.

"Attending the hot dog roast. I mean, he normally doesn't bother with *youngie* events." She frowned at Leah. "This could be a problem."

"Why a problem?" asked Leah.

Rachel glanced at her sister, then back at Leah. "Um, nothing." She turned toward the house. "Come, we'll show you around the house."

Leah frowned at the young woman's blatant attempt to sidestep the subject. There were undercurrents here she didn't understand. But one thing was certain. The last thing Leah wanted was to be a cause of strife within her host family.

Chapter Three

Back in the house, Rachel offered Leah a brief tour around the inside before joining her mother and sisters in the kitchen.

Edith mixed something in a large bowl. "If you're going down to the cellar, fetch some *flaisch brieh* while you're there."

"Ja," agreed Rachel.

Flaisch brieh. The term was unfamiliar to Leah.

"Green beans," clarified Edith, noticing her confusion.

Rachel opened a door in the wall of the kitchen to reveal steps leading down to a basement. It was not pitch-dark since a little light came from small high windows in the house's foundation. When Leah descended to the concrete floor, cool on her bare feet, she saw wide double doors with windows leading to a ramped driveway.

"In case we need to back the wagon up after a harvest," Rachel explained, pointing to the doors. "We can unload through those doors. Plus it gives us a bit of natural light."

As her eyes adjusted, Leah made out stacked wooden bins, stacked plastic buckets, and what seemed like miles of shelves. "What's all this?"

"Food, mostly." Rachel pointed. "Buckets of wheat and rice, beans, corn. We use plastic buckets because it keeps the mice out. We get the buckets secondhand from grocery store bakery departments. These are the shelves of our home-canned food." In the gloom, hundreds of glass jars twinkled.

"You won't starve, that's for sure."

"We've had a couple of winters when the snow was very deep," Rachel recalled. "Everyone preserves their harvest and keeps it in their cellars." A lilt of suppressed mirth entered her voice. "It's not like we can dash to the grocery store in our car." She chuckled, and Leah joined in. The very thought seemed strange.

Rachel walked to one shelf and withdrew two quart jars of green beans, one of which she handed to Leah.

"You canned these yourself?"

"*Ja*, sure, from last summer's garden."

The journalist in her asked, "How many quarts of beans do you can each summer?"

"About a hundred or so, give or take. We try to put up enough to have a vegetable with each meal rotating every week for a year. If we eat green beans just once a week and have two quarts at the meal, then we only need about a hundred quarts to last us through the year. That's our minimum amount, but of course we'll preserve whatever bounty *Gott* gives us."

Drawing the logical conclusion, Leah observed, "I'll bet harvest time is very busy."

"*Ja*, sure. But it's also a lot of fun, everyone working together. The garden also keeps us busy throughout the summer. I hope you'll join us in some of the work."

"Of course. I want to help however I can, but you'll have to teach me the difference between a weed and a carrot."

Rachel paused, the quart of beans cradled in one arm. "What's it like, living in the city?"

How to answer such a question? In just the few hours she'd been here, it was clear the Bylers could never understand the complexities of urban life, from navigating the best commuting route to selecting the perfect outfit from the closet, or the constant pressure of checking her smartphone.

"Complicated," she answered at last. "Everything is more complicated. Prices are higher, roads are crowded, there's noise everywhere. The day before this happened—" she gestured toward her face "—I would have said nothing could pry me away from the city or my job. I thrived on the chaos and competition, the television ratings and chasing a news lead. Then…" Her voice cracked. "Then it all came crashing down in one moment."

"What happened?" In the gloom of the basement, Rachel's expression was compassionate.

Leah sighed. "I was filming a story on gang violence in LA. It was the night of January first, New Year's Day, a cold night out on the streets. I saw two gang members kill a woman and her child. They just knifed them down in cold blood."

Rachel gasped.

"They didn't see me or my cameraman, and we filmed the whole thing." Leah's voice trembled. "I'll never forget it. It was pure accident they were killed on camera, and it happened so fast neither of us could have stopped it. But they saw us. Suddenly we were running for our lives down a dark alley. They caught up with us when I tripped and fell."

Rachel gulped. "What then?"

"One…one of them started slashing my face. I thought he was going to slit my throat, but my cameraman, Ted, kicked him in the head so he was knocked out. Ted saved my life that night. He decked the other guy, dragged me to my feet, and we made it back to the news van and got out of there. He took me straight to the hospital, where they had to do some reconstruction work on me, but it was clear from that moment my career in front of the camera was over."

"How long were you in the hospital?"

"A week. My station aired the footage of the murders, and from then on I've been hunted. They had to post a guard at my hospital room door after some people tried to get in. I wasn't safe at my apartment. It took no time for my address to become known. They want me dead. Finally the authorities put me in witness protection, which is how I ended up here, through the kindness of your parents. Since I speak a little bit of German, that was a factor in choosing the Amish. That, and the sheer distance from Los Angeles."

Rachel collapsed against one of the shelving units, and her breath whooshed out. "So that's what it's like, living in a city."

"No. Thankfully it's not, or no one would live in a city. I was just in the wrong place at the wrong time.

But it's not safe for me to go back. Not now, not with how well I'm known in the area."

"But what will you do after this? After your stay with us is over?"

"I don't know." Leah looked at the jar in her hands. "Learn how to can green beans, I guess."

Back upstairs, Sarah had joined her mother and younger sister in the kitchen, chopping vegetables. Edith took the jars of beans and put them on the counter, and without a word Rachel took up a knife and began working too.

"What can I do?" Leah lingered by the basement door. "And what are you making?"

"A casserole you can take to the hot dog roast tonight." Edith picked up a glass baking dish. "I'm making two, actually, one for ourselves and one for you to take. We'll just have Ivan and the younger *kinner* home for supper, so one casserole dish will be plenty for us for a meal. Would you like to peel some potatoes?" She gestured toward the sink, where a small basket of potatoes rested. "Here's a peeler."

Leah stood at the sink and peeled. The youngest sister, Eliza, noticed her technique. "Um, would you like to know a little trick to make it go faster?"

"Sure."

"Like this." The girl took the spud and the peeler and whipped the skin off the vegetable with speedy outward movements. "Try it."

Embarrassed to be schooled by such a young child, Leah took the peeler and imitated the girl's confident, rapid technique. Sure enough, she finished the potato within a few seconds. "Thank you!"

Behind her, Edith chuckled. "I hope she didn't offend. Many things are learned while very young, and it's hard not to share."

"I'm not offended." Leah reached for another potato. "If you don't mind the fact that I'm a novice in the kitchen."

For the next half hour, Leah worked with the other women until the casseroles were constructed to Edith's satisfaction. "There, that's ready." She glanced at a clock over the sink. "There's time to work in the garden before you go. I'll take care of the kitchen."

The daughters washed their hands and headed for the back door. Leah trailed after them, wondering in the back of her mind how much downtime anyone ever got. Already she'd done more domestic chores in the space of a few hours than she normally did in a week.

The girls grabbed small tools from a box near the garden gate. Rachel pointed. "Look, Isaac is still here. I thought he'd gone home by now."

Leah saw Isaac in conversation with Ivan outside the shop. "He said he had a little more work to do."

"*Ja*, maybe." Rachel turned and plopped down amid the rows of vegetables.

Leah squatted next to her. "Which are weeds and which are vegetables?"

"See these?" Rachel pointed to rows of wispy, delicate vegetation. "These are carrots. Anything that doesn't look like this should come out. Here, use my weeder. I'll go get another." She handed Leah a tool that looked like a screwdriver with a notched end.

Leah dug the tool into the ground to lever out the weed roots, then pulled the plant. She got the hang of it within one minute and kept up as the Byler girls worked their way down the rows of carrots.

"This is fun!" she exclaimed, eliciting chuckles from the others.

"I like weeding," Rachel said. "It makes everything look so neat and tidy. Like *haus* cleaning, only in the garden. And don't worry, you'll learn as you go. It's not like there's a test or anything."

Leah warmed to the short woman. Rachel twinkled with irrepressible humor and good cheer. "Thanks. I don't want to be a drag."

"Need help?" Isaac asked from behind.

Sarah turned. "Since when do you work in the garden?"

"Since I don't have much else to do this afternoon."

Leah saw Sarah exchange a lightning glance with her sister. "The tools are by the garden gate. Help yourself."

To Leah's surprise, he did. Like those of the Byler girls, his movements were swift and efficient.

With so many hands, the weeds didn't stand a chance. The sun wasn't too hot, the earth smelled fresh and moist, the birds sang around them, and Leah was enjoying herself more than she thought possible.

"If I were in Los Angeles right now," she mused, "I'd be working on a computer. Or maybe driving with a news crew to cover a story. The last thing I'd be doing is weeding carrots in the bright sunshine on a lovely afternoon."

"Why aren't you married?" asked young Eliza, with the candor of youth.

"Shh, *schtupid*, that's not polite!" hissed Rachel, glaring at her sister.

Leah didn't take offense. "I've dated, but I've always been more focused on my career than my personal life."

"But no *kinner*," mourned Sarah.

Leah's good humor started to dissipate. How to explain that children weren't even on her radar? "Maybe not, but there's still time." She poked her tool into the ground.

"Maybe you'll find a *hutband* here," observed Eliza.

"Impossible," replied Rachel. "She's not Amish."

She noticed that Isaac stayed silent in the face of this conversation, levering weeds out of the soil.

Leah became curious over Rachel's comment. "How often do outsiders become Amish?"

"Not very often." Sarah rubbed her cheek and left a smear of dirt. "Most don't like living without cars or telephones."

"But you do?"

"Well, on my *rumspringa* I had some excitement but decided it wasn't for me. I wanted to come back and be baptized right away." Sarah's lovely face glowed with health and beauty as she glanced over the garden. "I decided cars weren't any better than walking on foot, and grocery stores don't have any good food in them."

Leah refrained from informing Sarah about other attractions of the modern world. It was not her place to make the Bylers' oldest daughter question her faith or her community.

"That's how you felt, too, right, Isaac?" asked Sarah.

"*Ja*, sure. It's why I came back."

"Besides." Rachel pulled a weed. "On my *rumspringa*, I missed having friends around all the time. It seems a lot of *Englisch* people are lonely. I know I would be, if I didn't have the church community around me all the time."

The words were simply spoken, but they made Leah blink hard for a few moments. Short or not, Rachel knew where she belonged. She had a place in this community. She knew what her role was in life.

Where do I belong? Leah had a moment of profound loneliness. She belonged nowhere. She no longer knew what her role was in life. She was rootless, without the community or even faith that sustained these three daughters of the Byler family.

What would it be like to be so unquestionably accepted? Leah had clawed her way to the top for so long that the thought of sinking quietly into a society that accepted its members with love and loyalty was intriguing.

All those years of work—high school, college, internships, career, ratings, recognition—had been snatched away in a few minutes by two evil men, which was how she found herself wearing an apron and *kapp* and weeding carrots. Life was so *unfair* at times.

"Regrets?" murmured Isaac from nearby.

The man had an uncanny ability to read thoughts. "Some. It's hard not to sink down in self-pity."

"It'll get better. Trust in *Gott*."

A flash of anger made her snap, "Easy for you to say. You have no idea what I had to give up."

"Whatever it was, you're here now. Why fight it?"

"Because I'm a fighter. That's the only way to get ahead in life."

He raised his brows. "Who taught you that?"

"My mother." She clapped a hand over her mouth. She didn't mean to say that.

"Your mother?"

"Look, just drop it, will you?"

"I will, for now. But it sounds like there's a story behind that. I want to hear it."

You won't, she promised to herself. The man was entirely too intuitive as it was.

Sarah rose to her feet and dusted off her dress. "It's probably time to get ready. Isaac, *vielen dank* for your help."

"I'll see you at the hot dog roast, then." He rose, touched his hat and walked out of the garden.

Rachel stared after him. "How strange. He's never worked in our garden before."

"Nee." Sarah glanced at Leah. "I wonder why he did that?"

"Because he's nosy." Leah didn't want anything to do with Isaac Sommer. "I think I'll skip the hot dog roast. It's been a long day."

The sisters exchanged looks. "Are you sure?" asked Sarah. "Everyone is curious to meet you."

"But if Isaac is planning on being there…"

"So now you're a coward?" Rachel's tone was mild but her blue eyes held a challenge.

Leah clenched her fists. The taunt stung. "Okay, I'll go."

Chapter Four

Half an hour later, with the hot casserole packed in an insulated carrier, Leah set off with Sarah and Rachel toward the Miller farm, which Sarah told her was only a mile away.

A mile. In bare feet. In Los Angeles, no one walked a mile, let alone barefoot. They got into their cars and drove. Everywhere.

But the two young women didn't consider it anything odd. Swinging the food carrier, Sarah chattered about a young man named Aaron. "He'll be taking over his *daed*'s farm soon. He's the youngest of the family, so he inherits the farm."

"That's odd." Leah winced as she trod on a sharp stone. "I would have thought that older sons would inherit."

"No, they buy new farms, with their parents' help. Traditionally the home farm goes to the youngest boy."

"And where will Aaron's parents live, when Aaron takes over the farm?"

"Oh, nearly all farmhouses have a *daadi haus* attached for older parents. They're often relieved to move in there and leave the hard farmwork to the younger generation."

"So if the baby your mother is carrying is a girl, then the farm will eventually go to your youngest brother?"

"*Ja.* And if it's a boy, it will go to him."

"And none of the older boys are upset about this?"

Both girls looked at Leah in surprise. "No, of course not. Why would they be?" said Rachel. "All young men learn a trade or get help buying another farm, if that's what they want to do. If things get too crowded around here, some people leave to form a new church elsewhere."

"I see." It seemed so neat and tidy, somehow. No wonder the Amish were flourishing.

"So are you marrying Aaron?" she asked Sarah.

The lovely young woman blushed. "As *Gott* wills," she murmured.

"We don't normally discuss such things out in the open," advised Rachel. "Though it's well known I've decided not to marry, even if I found someone willing to marry me. I shall teach school instead." Her voice betrayed no sorrow or bitterness, just an acceptance of God's will.

"Do Amish women teach?" asked Leah.

"*Ja*, of course, who do you think teaches our children?"

"I thought they went to public school."

"They did, long ago, but fortunately we now have our own schools."

"Aren't you quite young to be a schoolteacher?"

"Not especially. I've already spoken to the bishop,

and the school board has accepted my application. I'll start in the fall with the current teacher, and she'll help guide me for a year or two."

"And will you continue to live at home while you teach?"

"*Ja.* I can easily walk to the schoolhouse—it's where Sarah and I went to school, and where our younger siblings go now."

Leah sighed. "I'm older than you, and yet you both have your lives already planned out. But I'm rudderless at the moment."

She detected a hint of surprise from both girls. "Put your trust in *Gott*," suggested Rachel. "He's the only one who can plan your life. Not you."

Leah digested this notion. To her, God was a shadowy figure, a vague Being who didn't have much to do with what happened in her everyday life. She hadn't grown up with any meaningful religious practice, so putting her trust in God was a very foreign concept.

"Look, there's Hannah." Sarah waved to a group of distant figures coming down an adjacent lane. "And Mark and Matthew with her."

"The Yoder family," Rachel explained to Leah. "They're about our age."

The other group of young people met them at an intersection and launched into *Deitsch* chatter, a little of which she understood but most of which was unintelligible. Leah noticed their eyes darting toward her.

Finally Rachel spoke in English. "This is our friend Leah Porte," she introduced. "She's staying with us for a few months. She's not Amish." Rachel pointed. "This is Matthew Yoder. Mark Yoder. Hannah Yoder."

One by one, each of the young people stepped forward and pumped Leah's hand.

"Kannscht du Deitsch schwetze?" asked Hannah.

Leah caught the gist. "No, I speak a little High German but not *Deitsch*," she replied.

"Then we will speak English," responded Matthew.

"Thank you."

Walking again, the Yoders fell in with Leah and the Byler girls. "Why are you visiting?" Hannah asked.

The forthright question was not meant to be rude, Leah knew. She decided to spread the same story she'd told Isaac. "I was in a bad car accident a few months ago." She touched her cheek. "I can't go back to my former job, and the Bylers gave me a place to stay for a little while."

All three Yoders nodded with apparent understanding. "We're glad you are here." Hannah spoke simply.

Leah felt her throat thicken. Despite the culture and language differences, despite her scarred face, no one she had met yet had been anything but very welcoming. "Thank you," she mumbled.

Conversation turned to who the younger people hoped would be at the gathering. Leah tried not to feel left out. It was clear the Bylers and Yoders had known each other since infancy and were perfectly comfortable in each other's company.

She was beginning to see something of the strength the Amish forged through their strong ties with each other. They didn't compete; they cooperated. They didn't tear down; they built up. Rachel, so much shorter than her companions, was clearly just as loved and accepted as Sarah with all her beauty.

"Big group." Mark pointed.

Leah looked over a field and saw a white farmhouse ringed with outbuildings and trees. Smoke rose, and people in colorful garments milled about.

"Come on, I don't want to miss anything." Sarah picked up her pace.

Normally not a shy person, Leah felt like hanging back as they approached the crowd. People called greetings, and everyone stopped to stare at her for a second or two—not because of her scar, she realized, but because she was a stranger.

An older couple approached her. "Miss Porte?" asked the man, smiling through his bushy white beard. "I'm Abram Miller. This is my wife, Charity."

"How do you do?" Leah received a strong hand pump from both. "Thank you for letting me come."

"We thought you might. Most people are aware the Bylers have you staying with them." From the sharp expression on both their faces, Leah suspected the Millers knew more than the bland story she was telling people and understood she was in witness protection.

"Most people here are *youngies*," Charity Miller said, "so we thought you might like to sit with us and some of the older folks while the younger ones eat and play games."

"Thank you, I'd like that." Leah warmed to the couple. "I think Sarah has a casserole."

"She knows where to put it. Come along now, we will introduce you to some people."

What followed was an extraordinary evening for Leah. Having never seen a large group of teens and young adults romp and sing and play games in such a—the word *wholesome* sprang to mind—manner, she expressed her admiration to her hosts.

"They're a good group of *youngies*," beamed Charity, spooning some salad from her plate. "Ah, here's Isaac. *Gut'n owed*, Isaac."

Leah's heart gave a thump as she looked up to see her acquaintance of this afternoon approach. She kept her voice steady. "Hello, Isaac."

He thumbed the brim of his hat and grinned at her, plopping down uninvited by Abram. *"Gut'n owed."*

"You've met?" Abram sounded surprised.

"Ja, sure, since I'm working with Ivan for the next few months. I gave Leah the farm tour this afternoon."

"And Ivan's story will be next in your magazine?"

"Ja." Isaac rubbed his chin and glanced at Leah, though he directed his words to Abram. "Leah tells me she worked as a reporter and can write articles. She may do some things for the magazine while she's here."

"I said nothing of the sort," Leah snapped. "You're making assumptions."

"You'll change your mind." He grinned with maddening confidence.

"Isaac once printed a poem of mine." Charity interrupted the argument. "But I could never write a whole story."

"You just haven't tried," admonished Isaac in what was clearly an established case on his part.

Despite her stubborn resistance, the journalist in Leah felt curious. "What's the circulation of your magazine?"

"About ten thousand," he replied. "I'm trying to increase the numbers, of course, mostly to Plain People in the various states."

"I'd like to see a copy."

"*Ja*, I'm sorry, I meant to bring one this afternoon. I'll bring one with me tomorrow."

"Don't rush. I'm not going anywhere." She took a bite of her strudel. "Do you work by an editorial calendar?"

"Roughly. I don't adhere to it too strictly, and of course I keep seasonal subjects in mind."

"And it's about farming?"

"Yes. And rural businesses, and rural lifestyles and other things of interest to Plain People."

"It's no wonder I haven't seen an issue in Los Angeles." She gave a ghost of a smile.

"So far away," murmured Charity. "This must be a very different place for you."

"It is. But I like it here so far." She gazed over the scene. The Millers had set up tables, which groaned under all the food. A shallow pit, about fifteen feet long and one foot wide, held an elongated campfire. Dozens of chattering, laughing young people were sitting or standing around the fire, holding hot dogs speared on prongs and roasting them over the flames and coals. Occasionally snatches of song rose up and floated on the warm June evening.

Leah spotted Sarah sitting next to a young man she presumed was Aaron. They talked animatedly together but didn't touch. She began to realize public displays of affection were discouraged among the Amish.

Something caught her eye. "Oh—what's that?" she gasped.

"What?" All eyes turned toward her pointing finger.

In the growing darkness, magical sparkles floated over the fields and lawn.

"Those!" exclaimed Leah. "Those lights!"

The Millers and Isaac all burst out laughing. "Those are *glühwürmchen*. Fireflies," chuckled Isaac. "Haven't you ever seen them before?"

"No!" One flew near her. Feeling like she was reaching for a fairy, Leah rose from her seat and caught the insect in her cupped hands. She examined it. It was plain, yet it was beautiful. It was a metaphor, she realized, for the Amish. Plain, but beautiful. "They're amazing!"

"I heard they don't have fireflies in the west," commented Charity. "So sad."

Leah released the insect. It crawled to the edge of her hand, spread its wings and took off, its tail end glowing on and off.

"I've never seen anything like it!" Feeling a bit like she was glowing herself, Leah stared after it, then resumed her seat. "I think I'm going to like it here."

Abram laughed. "Those fireflies, they are all over on summer evenings. We take them for granted, but you're right, they're *wunderschönen*. Sometimes it's good to be reminded of *Gott*'s wonders."

With the Amish, everything came back to God, Leah realized. She recalled Rachel's earlier comment about how she should put her trust in Him. "He's the only one who can plan your life. Not you," Rachel had said.

Even, it seems, in matters of appreciating fireflies.

But she couldn't do it. God just didn't seem real to her.

She listened as Abram and Isaac talked about the Millers' dairy and how the animals were doing.

This, too, was new and different for her. She was used to colleagues discussing career issues—which was exactly what Abram and Isaac were doing. But what very different careers, and very different issues.

She found herself smiling. Charity asked her, "What's so funny?"

"Just contrasting my old life with this one," she replied.

"It must be very different." The older woman paused. "Just so you know, Edith told us the whole story of why you're here. You can depend on our silence."

Leah stole a lightning glance at Isaac, but he was engrossed in conversation with Abram. "Thank you. I hate lying, but I'm sure you understand why it's necessary."

"Ja." Charity nibbled a biscuit. "I can't imagine being worried for my life."

"Count your blessings."

"Oh, I do, my dear. Daily."

By the time the party broke up, it was pitch-dark and the stars shone overhead with a brilliance Leah had never, ever seen. The fireflies were starting to peter out, as well.

Yawning, Sarah walked over to the Millers to thank them for hosting. Aaron trailed behind. "Leah, this is Aaron. Aaron, Leah Porte."

Aaron was a pleasant-looking young man with blond hair and blue eyes. He pumped Leah's hand, but it was clear his vision was filled with the sight of the lovely young woman beside him.

"Sunday?" Sarah asked Aaron.

"Sunday," he agreed, clearly acknowledging a previous arrangement. He flicked his hat brim and moved off.

Groups of chattering young people departed in all directions. Leah thanked the Millers for their hospitality and fell in with the Byler sisters.

And Isaac.

"I'll walk back with you." He directed his words at all the young women.

Leah caught a look exchanged between Sarah and Rachel. "Thank you," said Rachel.

They set off down the dark road, lit only by starlight and a half-moon high in the sky. The sisters padded ahead, chatting in *Deitsch*. Walking behind them with Isaac felt unsettling to Leah, almost as if they were on a date.

"This must have been quite an eventful first day for you," he commented. "So many new things to see and do. And people to meet."

"Yes. It's going to take me some time to adapt, but everyone's been so kind and welcoming."

"Why won't you write for my magazine?" he blurted.

She sighed. "Look, as you just said, I've only been here one day. I don't know why you're pushing so hard."

"Maybe it's because I seldom get to meet a—a colleague of sorts. If you were as big a name as you said in Los Angeles, then it's apparent you have a lot of talent and you could only benefit the publication."

"That's rather mercenary on your part, isn't it?"

He remained silent for so long that Leah stole a look at him, dim in the starlight. "What's wrong?"

"You're right," he admitted. "It was mercenary on my part. Prideful. I was thinking only of the magazine, not you."

A little part of her melted. "Then let's change the

subject. Forgive me, but how is it you're using a computer and a camera? I thought those things were forbidden to the Amish."

"It took some persuasion, I'll admit," he replied. "It helps that we're a modern order—"

"What do you mean, 'modern order'? Edith used that term too. I thought the Amish were the Amish."

"No, not at all. Groups tend to interpret modern conveniences differently. The Old Order groups live very differently than the Beachy groups, which even drive cars. We're not as modern as that, but the bishop liked the idea of a magazine geared toward Plain People, so long as I could produce it in a way that was not disruptive to our way of life. I'm walking something of a fine line, trying to show I'm not out to corrupt anyone but merely to serve *Gott* with the gifts I'm given."

His casual reference to his faith disturbed Leah, who still felt God—if He existed—had a lot of explaining to do when it came to changing her life so completely last January. In her momentary lapse into bitterness, she lost the train of Isaac's conversation.

"So if you're agreeable," Isaac was saying, "perhaps on Friday you can show me what I'm doing wrong."

"I'm sorry," she apologized. "Show you what?"

"I'm having some trouble with the computer software. I'm hoping you might know what I'm doing wrong."

"Well, I'm no expert, but I guess I can take a look."

"*Gut.* It's been a stretch for me, learning how to use a computer, but people seem to like the magazine, so I think I'm doing well." There was the barest hint of uncertainty in his voice.

"Has it been a difficult adjustment, coming back?"

"Oh, so you know?"

"Edith and Ivan told me you spent some years away from Pikeville."

"It's no secret." He rubbed his chin. "*Ja*, it was difficult. I had too many *Englisch* ways in the beginning, but I've tried to forget them. The outside world… I liked it at first. I liked it too much. But it strips away a man's faith and tries to replace it with other things. Competition, power, ambition. And technology. Technology has so many uses, but it drives many things away."

"Like what?" Having grown up with nothing *but* competition, power, ambition—not to mention technology—she wasn't sure she wanted to hear a litany of woe. But the journalist in her asked the question.

"Like this." He gestured ahead at Sarah and Rachel, then at the dark landscape around them. "When I lived with the *Englisch*, no one liked to talk, to walk anywhere. They like brightly lit places with loud noises and loud music. I went to a movie once and the sound—the soundtrack—was so loud I had my fingers in my ears almost the whole time."

"What movie?"

"Jurassic Park."

"Oh, good movie."

"It was impressive to see dinosaurs stomping around." He grinned. "They were so huge on the screen…it was like they were come to life." In the starlight, she saw his grin fall. "But it made me feel guilty too. We shun movies and television and cameras. Seeing a movie, even an older movie, made me feel I was supporting an industry we don't approve of. And as for using a camera for the magazine…" He trailed off.

"I suppose I can see the conflict."

"It's been a problem. Then I came back home and found myself between two cultures. No one here knows what *Jurassic Park* is. Or even wants to."

"But you *did* come back."

"Yes. The benefits of returning home outweighed the detriments of staying away. I couldn't give up my faith. *Gott* has been too good to me to turn my back on Him. Look, they're expecting you…"

Leah looked ahead and saw an oil lamp set in a windowsill of the Bylers' living room. It was a charming sight.

As if on cue, Sarah turned. "*Danke schön*, Isaac. *Gut nacht.*"

He tapped his hat brim. "*Bitte schön.*" Without further ado, he turned and walked away into the darkness.

Leah stared after him. "Does he have a long way to go?"

"*Nein*, just a mile or so." A yawn split Sarah's face. "I'm tired… I'm off to bed."

The house was silent. Rachel took the lamp off the windowsill and showed Leah where the bathroom was. It seemed odd to wash up by lamplight, but she felt refreshed afterward.

Rachel carried the lamp upstairs and into Leah's room. "Here, light your own lamp," she said, "before I take this one away."

Leah bit her lip. "I've never lit an oil lamp before."

Rachel's eyes widened in surprise, but she didn't

say a word of reproach. "Like this." She put down the lit lamp.

She went through a brief instructional on removing and replacing the chimney, touching the match sideways to the wick, and lowering the wick to the proper height. "Never leave off the chimney," she said. "It regulates the air flow. If you leave off the chimney when the lamp is lit, it can overheat and pressurize the lamp base and might catch fire. To blow out the lamp, cup your hand over the chimney like this—" she demonstrated "—and blow into your hand, so the air is directed down into the chimney. Don't try to remove the chimney while the flame is going or you'll burn your hand."

Leah nodded, hoping she would remember all the details and—more important—that she wouldn't burn the house down.

Then Rachel was gone, leaving Leah to the quiet bedroom.

A white cotton nightgown, utterly unadorned, hung from one of the clothes hooks. The bedroom window was open, and she heard the sound of crickets. Closing the simple sheet curtain over the window—not that she needed much privacy out here in the middle of nowhere—she removed her *kapp* and dress and donned the nightgown, which slithered all the way to the floor.

Then she sat on the bed and looked at the pretty glowing lamp and wondered what on earth she was doing here—and what to expect next. She heard the crickets and nothing else—no car horns, no sounds of traffic, nothing of the indefinable rumble of urban life. No hum of electrical devices, no blare of radios or televisions, no people talking in the corridor outside her apartment door. Nothing but crickets.

She touched the scar on her cheek. No one had mentioned it tonight at the hot dog roast, and there were times she actually forgot about it. But it was there, lumpy and red. Sometimes it ached. The doctors had done a nice job sewing it up, but there was only so much they could do. Perhaps someday she would be able to disguise it with makeup, but in her heart she knew it could never be disguised well enough to resume her job in front of a camera.

Okay, so she could work *behind* the camera. She'd been resisting the thought, in part because camera recognition fed her hungry ego, but recognition was now a deadly factor she could no longer risk. She literally didn't dare show her face in Los Angeles again…or anywhere else, for that matter.

So here she was, living anonymously in an isolated Amish community. It was the best place for her, she knew, and she would do her best to blend in.

For now.

Chapter Five

Leah heard a knocking at her door. "Leah, are you awake?"

"Hmm?" She opened her eyes to bright sunshine and birdsong coming in through the window. She felt disoriented. Where was she?

The bedroom door opened and Eliza poked her head inside. "Good morning, sleepyhead. It's late. Time to get up."

Leah realized she wasn't in her LA apartment; she was in Ohio.

"I must have overslept," she mumbled, trying to be gracious in her grogginess. It had taken her a long time to fall asleep last night.

"Breakfast is ready. *Mamm* sent me to get you."

"Thanks. I'll be right down."

Eliza closed the door, and Leah swung her feet out of bed. The birdsong poured through the window, the likes of which she'd never heard before. She peeked out, hoping to catch a glimpse of the source of this magical sound, but the thick leaves of the maple trees on the side of the house disguised the avian inhabitants.

Not wanting to keep the Bylers waiting, she wiggled as best she could into her clothes, stretching behind her back to reach the snaps. She twisted her hair into a bun and jammed it with pins, then fastened her *kapp*. Without a mirror, she hoped she looked presentable.

Snatching up her apron, she donned it as she exited her room and trotted downstairs. "Sorry I'm late," she panted, wondering what time it was. "It's not like me to oversleep."

"Good morning," said Edith and Ivan at the same time. If they were annoyed, they gave no hint of it with their broad smiles.

Leah seated herself and bowed her head as the family silently prayed. Then chatter broke out as Edith scooped food for the youngest children and Ivan passed around bowls of eggs and biscuits.

The food was incredible—biscuits and gravy, scrambled eggs, bacon, sausage, milk, coffee. Everything but the coffee, she suspected, came off the farm. "I'm going to have to watch out or I'll gain weight," she said between mouthfuls.

"Oh, you'll work it off," replied Edith. "Most people do."

"What time do you leave for the office?" she quipped to Ivan, who smiled.

"I'm rushing to finish an order for a store in Cleveland," he answered. "That's why I'm so glad Isaac is helping me. Sales have been slow lately, and this order will help a lot. They'll be sending a truck a couple weeks from now, so I have to make sure everything's finished before then."

"How many pieces are they taking? And what kind?"

"Four dressers and two beds."

"You must be very proud of your work."

Ivan looked at his plate. "The Lord has given me some skill," he mumbled.

Leah could have kicked herself. Pride—the Amish avoided it like the plague. "I'm sorry."

"We have laundry to do today, since we didn't do a load yesterday," Edith chimed in, helping to cover the awkward pause. "And baking."

Despite her mother's teaching that modern women didn't need domestic skills—not if they were pursuing a high-powered career—Leah felt anxious to redeem her blunder. "I'll be glad to help, but you'll have to show me how to do things."

"Of course."

She came to regret her offer—not that she could have, in good conscience, avoided making it. The Byler women worked, and worked hard. First came cleaning up the breakfast dishes, which—in the absence of a dishwasher—took a long time, though the women chatted cheerfully throughout. Then they broke into separate tasks. Edith and Eliza started dinner and began mixing dough for bread, while Sarah and Rachel hauled tubs onto the porch for laundry.

Leah offered to help with laundry. On a side porch, a large metal tub stood below a hand pump. The tub, Leah saw, was full of soaking clothes. Between two trees, metal clotheslines had six lines strung between them.

"How long have these been soaking?" she asked.

"Oh, about an hour or so," replied Rachel. "We mix up some detergent, put the clothes in and just let them sit. It helps get any stains out. Here, give me a hand with this, will you?"

"This" turned out to be a bulky, leggy contraption roughly shaped like a half barrel lying on its side, propped up on four stout legs. Leah helped carry it onto the porch. "What is it?" she asked.

"A washing machine," replied Rachel.

The wringer fastened to one end should have given Leah a clue, but since she'd never seen such a thing in real life, she wasn't certain. "How does it work?"

"Like this." Sarah dragged the washer toward the metal washtub. She lifted the Plexiglas cover and loaded clothes into the tub. From a bucket, Rachel scooped some slimy-looking gelatinous stuff that Leah presumed was detergent and plopped it over the clothes. Sarah started in pouring buckets of water, shut the lid and seized a handle at one end.

"All you do is swing this handle back and forth," she told Leah. "We're washing these in cold water, but we like to wash whites in hot water."

"Is that detergent?" asked Leah, pointing to the bucket of gelatinous goo.

"Yes, we made it ourselves," replied Rachel.

Of course they did. The list of self-sufficient skills the Bylers possessed was intimidating.

"How long do you swing the handle back and forth?" she asked Sarah.

"Here, you take a turn," she replied. "About eight minutes," she added.

Leah seized the handle. She felt the resistance as she

rocked it back and forth. "So let me guess, this agitates the clothes?"

"*Ja.* The movement kind of forces the water and detergent through the clothes. This load is pretty dirty, which is why we presoaked it. For less-dirty loads, we won't have to agitate as long."

"Clever," she admitted. "Even if it's more work than a regular washing machine."

When Sarah deemed the load clean, she drained the water through a plug hole at the bottom and added fresh water for a rinse. She repeated this again for a second rinse. Then Rachel fed the clothes through the wringer as Sarah cranked the handle and Leah caught the damp garments and put them in a basket.

"Want to help me hang?" asked Sarah as Rachel fished more dirty laundry from the tub into the washer.

"Sure."

"Here, grab a handle."

But Leah even needed instruction in this most elemental task, as she soon discovered.

"If you don't shake the clothes out, like this—" Sarah snapped a boy's shirt so it cracked "—then it will dry crumpled. Hang the shirt like this…" The lesson continued.

In the midst of this tutorial, Isaac came around the corner of the house. "*Guder mariye*, Sarah, Rachel." He flicked the brim of his straw hat.

Sarah looked around. "*Guder mariye*, Isaac."

Leah didn't want to admit the little jump she felt inside at the sight of him.

"I have a copy of the magazine for you, Leah." Isaac took an issue from under his arm.

Leah wiped her damp hands on her apron and took the magazine. "This looks professional."

He seemed pleased. "I hope so. It's been an uphill battle learning how to do everything."

She flipped through the contents, noting rural-themed subjects, which were appropriate, since the name—*Plain Farmer*—said it all.

It was illustrated with beautiful photographs. "Do you take all the photos? If so, I'm impressed."

"Most of them," he admitted. "Except when I get submissions from people elsewhere. Not all the subscribers are Plain. There are many people who just like rural life and who send in their contributions and their photos."

Leah chuckled. "Maybe you should cover a typical Amish laundry day."

"Maybe I should." He cocked his head. "Sometimes it's the little things that make the biggest impression."

"Hey, take it from someone who's never done laundry without electricity—it's not little." Not wanting Sarah to think her slacking, Leah placed the magazine on the grass beside the clothesline pole. She picked up a damp apron, snapped it and pinned it to the line.

"Anyway, are you still able to come over sometime and look at what I'm doing wrong with my computer?"

"I guess. Though I'm sure you understand I feel obligated to give my efforts to the Bylers, to help with their chores and such." She reached for a pair of boys' trousers. "They're the ones housing and feeding me."

"Talk it over with *Mamm*," advised Sarah from the other end of the clothesline. She kept her eyes on the garment in front of her. "She can let you know what needs to be done and when you might be able to get away."

"I'd best get to work, then. Ivan is expecting me." He flicked his hat brim and left.

"What does he want you to do with the magazine?" Sarah asked Leah while she fetched another article of clothing.

"He's pushing me to write for it, and I'm not interested. But he said he needs help troubleshooting on a computer program he uses."

"Do you know a lot about computers?"

"I'm no expert, but I know enough to get by. And I know a couple of desktop publishing programs, so I may be able to help him with that."

"Desktop pub… What did you call it? What's that?"

"Desktop publishing. It's when you do the layout of a document, such as a magazine, right there on the computer and then send it to a printer and they just print it off."

"Wow. You make it sound easy."

"It's not too hard. It's a lot better than the old days when everything was done by hand."

"Like laundry?" quipped Sarah, her blue eyes crinkling.

"Like laundry." Catching the humor, Leah took one handle of the now empty basket as Sarah took the other, and they walked to the porch, where Rachel was swinging the washer's handle on another load.

Laundry was just the first of many chores done that day. In the kitchen, preparations for lunch—which they called dinner—were well underway. An enormous bowl covered with a towel rested in a square of sunshine.

Eliza swept the entire downstairs of the house. Edith, waddling a bit with her girth, prepared a separate casserole for a neighbor who had just had a baby. Sarah offered to take the casserole over while Rachel worked in the garden.

"What would you like me to do?" asked Leah, feeling a little useless in the midst of all the industry.

"I'm sure Rachel would enjoy company in the garden," hinted Edith.

So Leah walked with Rachel to the garden and within minutes was involved in weeding beets and radishes.

"Word is spreading about you and Isaac," began Rachel without preamble.

"Word?" exclaimed Leah in alarm. "What do you mean?"

"I mean, he acts like a courting man."

Her jaw dropped. "But he can't be. We just met. And I'm not Amish."

"I know that. You know that. He knows that. It's a problem."

Leah yanked a weed. "I've only been here twenty-four hours. You're right, it's a problem." Then curiosity got the better of her. "So what does Amish courting even look like?"

"It's subtle, especially to someone not raised Amish, but to us it's screaming loud." Rachel smiled.

"He's barely met me."

"He's seen you more often than necessary. I guess that's one of the clues."

"But he works for your father."

"Yes, but he went to the hot dog roast last night, and he walked us home. Then today he dropped off a copy of the magazine. That's a lot in a twenty-four-hour period. And now you're going to work with him on his magazine."

"I'm *not* working with him on his magazine. I'm just looking at his computer problems." She knew her voice sounded cross. "Do you think I should avoid him?"

"No…no, not necessarily. And it sounds like you could help him a lot with his computer. Just be warned, though, he might be thinking of courting you."

A few moments of silence passed. "So why *isn't* he married?" Leah asked at last.

"I just don't think he can find a girl willing to take a chance on him. He has so much *Englisch* in him now."

"And that's a problem?"

"It is for a girl who's been baptized and prefers to stay wholly Amish."

"Well, I can tell you, no man will look twice at me anymore." The usual bitterness rose in Leah's throat.

"What? Why?"

"Why? Because of my face." She gestured in frustration. "Isn't it obvious?"

Rachel fixed her eyes on Leah. "There's nothing wrong with your face."

"You're right, except for this huge, livid scar that nearly slices me in half."

"Leah." The younger girl rested her busy hands for a moment. "You're angry, I can tell. But a face is just a face. Skin is just skin. You're still *you*, the person *Gott* created."

"But I can't do the job I was trained to do anymore."

"But you can do this job. Or you can work with Isaac on the magazine. Or you can do any other job you set yourself to. I don't pretend to know *Gott*'s mind, but maybe it's *Gott*'s will that you're here with us."

"God's will!" Anger flared. "You think it's God's will that I be scarred like this?"

"I think it's *Gott*'s will that I was born with a genetic disorder," replied Rachel gently.

Leah's anger drained. She'd had a lifetime of beauty, but Rachel had been dealing with her genetic stature since birth. "I'm sorry," she apologized. "You're right, I'm still angry."

"Have you taken your anger to *Gott*?"

"I thought He caused this to happen." She couldn't keep all the sarcasm out of her voice.

"Have you taken your anger to *Gott*?" repeated Rachel with a small smile. "Have you told Him you're angry? Have you asked Him how you can be healed? I don't mean healed on your face—I mean healed inside."

Leah kept her eyes on the weeds, yanking the unwanted plants with unnecessary force. "No," she admitted. "I don't know that it would do any good."

"I think you have what's sometimes called a *Gott*-shaped hole in your heart," commented Rachel, shifting to the next row of beets. "When someone has sorrow, they take their troubles to *Gott*. But if there's a hole inside where *Gott* should be, the hole gets filled with sorrow and it has no other place to go. It festers and gets infected, like a wound."

"And how do you fill this God-shaped hole?"

"You ask Him," said Rachel simply. "It's that easy."

"Is it? You certainly make it sound like it is."

"*Gott* doesn't throw complexities at us beyond our ability to cope. He means for it to be easy. Besides…"

Rachel rubbed her chin, leaving a small smear of dirt. "As you say, you've been here twenty-four hours now. How do you view me? Do you still see my dwarfism?"

Startled, Leah stared. "What do you mean?"

"I mean, we're having a nice conversation on a lovely June day while weeding a beautiful garden. You're not focused on the fact that my body is shaped differently, just like I'm not focused on the fact that your face has a scar. That's the way *Gott* works, you see. Within a short time of meeting someone, you see what they're like on the inside, not the outside. You don't see the outside imperfections, but the inside beauty."

She was right. Leah was so stunned she sat back and stared away across the garden for a moment. "So I'm making a bigger deal of this than anyone else is," she murmured, touching her cheek.

"It's normal for you to make a bigger deal. It's your face, after all, and from what you've said, it changed your career. But it didn't change you on the inside, except for being angry. And *Gott* can fix that, if you'll let Him." Rachel pulled a weed.

For a moment—just a moment—Leah felt an extraordinary feeling. It seemed like a wave washed over her, cleansing her of anger and bitterness and leaving peace in its wake.

Then she shook her head and the feeling passed. This was all too strange and bizarre for her. She resumed weeding, grateful for Rachel's soothing company but not yet willing—as the younger woman put it—to fill this so-called God-shaped hole in her heart.

But the memory of that feeling of purity lingered.

A clanging sounded in the distance. "Dinnertime,"

said Rachel, climbing to her feet and brushing her dress down. "I'm hungry, aren't you?"

"Yes. Actually I am." She stood up and looked at the rows of vegetables. "It looks good!"

"I've never minded weeding." Rachel chuckled and picked her way over rows of plants. "I like making things tidy."

Leah followed Rachel's example and washed her hands at the pump in the yard before going inside. Seeing the magazine she'd left by the clothesline, she picked it up and brought it indoors.

Isaac was in the kitchen with Ivan and the boys, washing up at the sink. With the family seated, all heads bowed in silent prayer. Leah mimicked the action, and for once she actually thought about the food before her. Seeing how hard everyone worked to grow, preserve and prepare it, maybe it *was* something to be thankful for. Inside, she made an effort to express gratitude.

"So what did you think of the magazine?" Isaac scooped some food onto his plate.

"I still haven't had a chance to look at it." Leah wagged a finger at him. "Are you being mercenary again?"

He grinned but didn't rise to the bait. Instead he directed a question at Edith. "Can you spare Leah later this afternoon? She said she'd look over a problem I'm having with my computer."

"We have butter to make, and some sewing." Edith adjusted her youngest son's booster seat. "Since you're not familiar with how to do those things, this afternoon is as good a time as any."

Leah felt her face heat up. She translated Edith's remark: *You're in the way.* She was definitely ignorant of most domestic duties. She got it.

"She thinks she's too good to write for me, but at least she's condescended to look at my computer." Isaac's tone was conversational, and he kept his face directed toward Edith.

"I'm sitting right here," Leah snapped. "You don't have to talk like I'm in the next room."

"Sorry. I wasn't sure if it was you sitting here, or your mother."

So he remembered her blunder from the garden yesterday in which she'd mentioned her mother. "What's that supposed to mean?"

"Nothing."

"Why are you deliberately pushing my buttons?"

"Because your eyes sparkle when you're annoyed."

His answer stopped her cold. She stared at him for a moment longer, then looked at her plate.

Ivan chuckled. "You two are like oil and water."

"Ja," agreed Isaac.

In all her professional life, Leah couldn't remember someone so simultaneously flirtatious and annoying. She didn't know what to make of him, and it left her feeling unsure of herself in a situation where she already felt like a fish out of water. She was tempted to skip the appointment but then remembered Rachel's soft accusation from yesterday. She clenched a fist and knew she would go.

After dinner, Isaac brought his plate to the sink. "Four o'clock?" he asked her. "I'll be done in the shop in an hour or so."

"I guess." She hated that she sounded ungracious.

"Danke." And he left.

Before departing, Leah sat down on the front porch steps and went through the magazine, noting its format and layout. It was a meaty journal without a lot of fluffy advertising. It opened with a table of contents and letters from readers, then launched into a mixture of philosophical essays, how-to instructions for splitting wood and storing potatoes, coverage of rural-themed events such as Horse Progress Days, interviews with businesses, even some poetry. She flipped through articles on shearing sheep and how to set the price for a buggy horse, a primer on growing garlic, some recipes…in short, whatever would interest people involved in small farming.

Despite the subject matter, she grasped what Isaac was getting at. He was attempting to unify a diverse set of rural inhabitants, everyone from the religious Amish to the free-spirited hippies, all bonded by a mutual love of nature and rural living, a do-it-yourself attitude, and a practical need to know more information. It wasn't something that appealed to her.

Armed with this insight, she put the magazine in her room, obtained directions from Edith and set out to walk to Isaac's house.

Her bare feet were still tender, so she kept to the side of the gravel road where grass softened the surface. The mile distance would take her about twenty minutes to walk, said Edith, and Leah couldn't help but compare walking a mile here in rural Ohio with walking a mile in urban Los Angeles. In the city, no one walked.

But no one saw what she saw either. Walking gave perspective, not speed. Tall grasses waved along the roadside. She smelled fresh earth from someone's plowed field. She heard birdsong and saw butterflies. She saw blue flowers and white flowers and yellow flowers and red flowers—and didn't know any of their names.

In the distance, a man in a straw hat and suspenders sat on the metal seat of some sort of farm contraption, pulled by two large horses, dragging an implement through the dirt of the field. Not far beyond, a big white farmhouse sported tire swings from two huge trees shading the yard, and two children apiece clinging to them, shrieking with laughter. She saw the unmistakable signs of a huge garden behind the house.

She didn't hear anything modern: no cars, no trains, no airplanes, no radios. Just birdsong, laughing children, and frogs croaking unseen in a ditch.

Everywhere she felt bucolic peace. Now she knew the scenery was the result of hard work by hard-working people, but that didn't make it any less lovely.

No, this wasn't a bad place to live…for a little while.

Chapter Six

As she walked, Leah tried not to feel annoyed at Edith for cornering her into agreeing to work with Isaac. The pregnant woman had a large household to run and many tasks to do. Having a clumsy, ignorant stranger messing up her efficiency couldn't be easy. So Leah would work with Isaac and stay out of her way.

It also lit a grim determination within her to conquer this new domestic frontier. For now, her journalism career was on hold. Maybe it was time to learn how to make butter.

Within twenty minutes, she saw Isaac's home. "Look for the white picket fence and a green mailbox," Edith had told her.

Sure enough, a picket fence lined the lawn with a shiny green mailbox at the road. As with most Amish homes, the building was large and white. A barn stood adjacent.

She walked up the pathway to the front door and knocked on the screen doorframe, trying not to peer through the open front door. After a minute or two, an older woman came to the door, wiping her hands on her apron. *"Guder nammidaag,"* she said. *"Vee bisht du hight?"*

Leah caught the gist. *"Guder nammidaag,"* she repeated. "Do you speak English?"

Surprise registered in the woman's eyes. *"Ja,"* she said.

"My name is Leah Porte. I'm here to see Isaac, if he's home."

"Ja. Please come in. My name is Eleanor Sommer. I'm Isaac's mother. You're the *Englisch* woman staying with the Bylers, no?"

"Yes. Isaac wanted to talk over some computer issues with me."

"This way." The older woman turned and led the way through a spacious living room to a kitchen not dissimilar to the Bylers'. She walked with a pronounced limp and sometimes reached out to steady herself on a wall or piece of furniture. "Please, sit," she said, gesturing to the kitchen table, then went to a back screen door. "Isaac!" she called toward the barn.

"Ja?"

"There is an *Englisch* lady here to see you!"

"All right!"

Eleanor turned back to the kitchen. "Would you like some tea?"

"Yes, thank you."

By the time Isaac came in carrying a computer case, Eleanor had poured hot water into two large mugs and tucked tea leaves into two strainers, which she dropped into the steaming water. She placed the mugs on the table, along with spoons and a sugar bowl.

"Thank you," said Leah. "Hi, Isaac."

"Edith didn't tie you up with too much work?" He dropped into the chair opposite her and reached for a cookie from the plate his mother placed on the table between them before leaving the room.

"I don't know how to sew or make butter, so no. I guess I'm more useful here." She meant the words to sound sarcastic, but instead they had an overtone of pathos she didn't intend.

"Don't be discouraged." To her surprise, he didn't tease. "This is all new to you, but it's nothing you can't learn."

"But in the meantime, it means I'm all thumbs."

"Except on a computer."

"Well…yeah." She dipped her tea strainer. "I suppose."

"So are you ready to look at this software program?"

"Sure." What else could she say?

He pulled a black laptop from his computer bag and set it on the table. While it booted up, she asked, "What program is giving you trouble?"

"InDesign. Are you familiar with it?"

"Yes, very." She straightened up. "It's a very common program, very versatile."

"I've had such a battle learning it."

"Do you do the whole layout of the magazine?"

"*Ja.* It takes me a long time." He angled the computer so she could see the screen. "Especially when it comes near the time to send it to the printers, sometimes I'm up all night."

Leah rubbed her chin. She didn't know how to make butter, she didn't know how to sew, she didn't know how to cook, she didn't know how to do the endless things the Byler women did daily—but she *did* know how to do desktop publishing. Maybe witness protection should have placed her here instead of with the Bylers.

"I can help you with the layout," she admitted. "I'm pretty fast on this program. If you have the format set up, half the job is already done."

He looked relieved. "What a shame you're not going to be here forever or I might just dump the whole thing on you."

"Why?"

"Because I like working on the magazine, but I don't like the computer work."

"There's nothing to it once you get the basics down. I've done more computer work in my time than I like to admit. I've done a lot less since…since my accident."

"Do you miss it?"

"The computer work? No. The rest of my job? Of course."

He nodded but didn't probe. "Well. I have my interview with Ivan ready to go for the upcoming issue. I just needed the photographs, which I took yesterday."

Leah looked at the laptop. The battery bar showed the device was fully charged. "If you don't have electricity, how do you charge your computer?"

"Well, ah, actually I charge it in the barn. I use a solar-powered milking machine, and the solar panel also charges the computer battery."

"Do you have a website and email address?"

"No website, but I've got email." He grinned, his eyes crinkling. "But I can only access the internet from the library in Pikeville."

"Sounds very un-Amish to me."

"It depends. We're a fairly modern order, as I said earlier. The Amish church, like most religions, has different levels of strictness, which is set by the local bishop and varies a lot from region to region. Some of the dairy farmers around here are allowed to use generators for their milking machines, since dairy is their primary income." He tapped the machine. "I charge the laptop during milking time, early morning and evening. Sometimes I hire freelance designers too. That's why I'd be interested in hiring you."

Now it was Leah's turn to be startled. "Hire me? No! I didn't say anything about money."

For a moment she caught his eyes, and she felt her heart speed up. Rachel said he might be interested in courting her. While the old-fashioned term grated on her urban ears, she saw what Rachel meant. She instinctively understood his interest in her was more than just professional.

She also recalled Rachel's views about her facial scar. Could it be that Isaac didn't notice it, as Rachel said?

Certainly she was attentive to his appearance. He was attractive, with curly hair and cheerful features, and he seemed confident and self-assured, except for his computer skills. He was an altogether good-looking man, and she wouldn't be human if she didn't feel a tug of interest.

But despite her dress and *kapp*, she was too aware of the cultural divide between them. She was modern, he was old-fashioned. It was a pity.

Anxious to break her train of thought, she blurted,

"So what kind of problems are you having on the program?"

He tapped some keys and pulled up the program. "Here and here. I can't figure out how to wrap the text around this odd-shaped diagram, and I don't know how to make a table from these figures."

For the next half hour, Leah walked him through the confusing details until he understood. "Thank you!" he exclaimed at the end.

"No problem." She leaned back and put some space between them. "I used this program every day when I was in college."

Isaac turned off the computer and shut the lid. "So what article do you want to write for me first?"

"I told you, I'm not." Whatever warm feelings she was feeling toward him dissolved in a puddle of frustration. "Please don't push, Isaac. I've got a lot on my plate at the moment and don't need anything else added."

He shrugged. "I'm not giving up. I think you have a lot to offer. Besides, look at it as a professional outlet for your skills."

Pain welled inside her. "My profession is dead to me at the moment! And you have a lot of nerve bringing it up."

He held up both hands as if stopping traffic. "Sorry. I didn't mean to rub a sore spot. I just thought having someone approach various subjects from the perspective of teaching something to those unfamiliar with the procedure would be helpful. Such as doing laundry without electricity."

Leah scrubbed a hand over her face. "I came from a position of competence and authority. I reported on high-ranking news scandals, regional disasters, and political events. And you want me to write about... laundry?"

His expression tightened. "So writing about laundry is beneath you?"

"I didn't say that."

"I'm Amish, not stupid, Leah. I caught the subtext just fine." His eyes flashed with anger.

"I'm just trying to be helpful. As for writing about laundry, forget it. You're right, it's beneath me."

"Then you're acting like a hypocrite."

She lifted her chin. "No, I'm not. I'm being honest."

"Then you were lying when you said you were interested in green and sustainable living. A zero-waste lifestyle. You say you support those things, yet you disdain the skills that make that kind of lifestyle possible. If those things are important to you, then you should be willing and able to preach it to others. And what better medium than my magazine?"

Leah's chest tightened. "It's not that I'm unwilling to write about those subjects. It's just that..."

"That what?"

"That this whole domestic thing isn't my cup of tea."

Surprise flattened his face. "Domestic thing? What are you talking about? We live here, Leah, doing what's necessary to live according to our principles. What's offensive about that? I'd really like to know."

Leah fiddled with the edge of her apron. The irony of fidgeting with such a feminine garment didn't escape her. "I was raised to believe women are strong and empowered individuals who are perfectly capable of competing with men in all aspects of the workplace. Stuff like laundry and sewing and other domestic skills just isn't on my radar."

His voice hardened. "Look, Leah, you're not in Los Angeles anymore. You're on a farm among a community of people who have a lot of work to do on a daily basis. The jobs you think you're too good for—laundry and sewing and cooking and such—are still jobs that must be done by *someone*. Women do them because most women don't want to do the physically harder jobs men do. No one is oppressing anyone. It's just the order of things."

"Seems like a mighty convenient order."

The flash of anger faded from his face. "I think I see the problem. You believe physical labor is something to be avoided. That's what modern conveniences are all about, right? Avoiding labor. That's why the *Englisch* world has washing machines and dishwashers and cars. But we believe in *gelassenheit*, which loosely translated means 'letting be.' We believe the earth should be left as close to *Gott*'s original creation as possible."

"Except when it comes to using a computer to lay out a magazine. Or solar panels to power milking machines. Sounds pretty hypocritical to me."

"If you're trying to provoke me, it won't work. I don't make up the rules of the *Ordnung*, I just follow them. We Amish must sift through modern conveniences to determine which ones will allow us to make a living in a modern world but without destroying the unity *Gott* gave us."

"It still seems backward."

He grinned, surprising her with the flash of humor. "I'm sure a lot of people believe exactly the same thing.

I think that's part of my interest in broadening the magazine's circulation—to show the Amish *aren't* backward, knuckle-dragging troglodytes or patriarchal oppressors—as some have hinted—but in fact have a lot to teach society. Not just in their approach to their carbon footprint, as you might put it, but by how their religious beliefs contribute to their overall peace of mind and lifestyle choices. Our beliefs are entwined with our lifestyle. There's no separating the two."

She accepted the olive branch and the change of subject with some relief. So far the people she'd met had been kind enough to take her in, and here she was letting her ego get in the way of a respectful discussion. "Does the magazine have Christian overtones? I didn't notice any when I glanced through the issue you dropped off this morning."

"Not per se. But for example, if someone wants to write on the subject, I wouldn't turn it down. Mostly it doesn't come up because it's just an accepted and understood facet of everyone's lives."

"So you don't evangelize on the street corner?"

"No. The Amish aren't evangelists in the sense of drawing outsiders in. Our spiritual life is mostly a personal thing, not expressed in public and not proclaimed loudly. The Bible says hypocrites love to stand on the street corners and pray loudly so they can be seen by others, but we're instructed to pray quietly and in secret. But since we're also instructed to spread the word, we tend to follow the 'straight stick' model of spreading the Gospel."

"Straight stick model? What's that?"

"Some might call it a form of evangelism. I guess it's

what the Amish use, when it comes down to brass tacks. Essentially you lay your straight stick next to someone else's crooked stick." He rubbed his chin. "Let's say someone has a troubled life or lacks a religious foundation or has made bad choices. Whatever the issue, they're missing the peace that *Gott* promises. Their lives are crooked sticks." He traced a warped line on the table. "Those who have that peace, and whose lives aren't troubled by bad choices, have straight sticks." He traced a solid line. "They don't have to preach at the troubled person—they just lay their straight stick next to the other person's crooked stick. The contrast is inescapable. So is the solution. Saint Francis of Assisi may have said it best—'Preach the gospel at all times, and when necessary, use words.'"

Leah was silent, thinking. "It's hard to argue with that," she admitted.

"Ain't so, right? In some ways, I think it accounts for some of the fascination for the Amish lifestyle. People don't just have a longing for, as you put it, a sustainable lifestyle. They also have a longing for the peace of *Gott*, which is a part of it. They just don't realize it. So when people look to the Amish for their sustainable, zero-waste lifestyle, by default they're also exposed to the strong religious convictions we live by. The two are inseparable, and it's what makes us what we are."

"That's all well and good, Isaac, but I don't see droves of people becoming Amish. And that includes myself."

"Can't give up the modern amenities you grew up with?"

"Of course not. I'm a modern woman and a product of my environment, despite the apron and *kapp* I'm wearing." She stood up. "I think it's time I go."

"You haven't finished your tea yet." Isaac knew it was time to switch tactics if he wanted to keep this fascinating woman involved with both him and the magazine. "I have to apologize. You've given me a lot of help, and I'm doing nothing but causing you grief. I'm sorry."

She hesitated, eyeing him, then dropped back into her seat. "You're an odd man, Isaac Sommer."

"So I've been told." He reached for another cookie, more for something to do than from hunger. "Finish your tea, at least, since there's no rush for you to get back to the Bylers."

"You mean I'm more useful when I'm out of their way?" To his relief, she smiled.

"Maybe." He smiled back.

Leah sighed. "I should apologize too. It's been a rough transition, from media darling to someone with a price on her head. And I still...still..." She gestured toward her scarred cheek, and he saw tears in her eyes. "I'm still adjusting to this."

"And it will take some time to recover. I realize that." He bit his cookie and spoke with his mouth full. "And no, I don't think you're being a hypocrite over the whole sustainable living thing. In fact, the longer you stay here, the more I think you'll enjoy the life we lead."

She leaned back in her chair, and he was pleased to see the interest reflected back in her expression. "What do you miss most about modern life? About the English world?"

"Books." He spoke without hesitation. "I read a lot

of books I might not otherwise read if I'd never left. Even now I have a bookshelf in my bedroom stuffed with many volumes I brought back with me. But I don't miss cars, I don't miss personal electronics, I don't miss the hustle and bustle." He sipped his tea. "But this is all new to you. What do *you* miss most about modern life?"

"Oh boy, that's a huge question. I've only been here a day, so I'm still trying to come to grips with all the changes and differences." She nibbled her cookie. "Off the top of my head, I'd say a lack of news is my biggest thing. I've been steeped in news for the last decade of my life, maybe even longer. It feels weird, not constantly monitoring the minute-by-minute changes in the political world. Now to be without radio or television or the internet makes me feel news deprived."

"I can understand that. It will be interesting to see if you feel the same way after two or three months. I found out the hard way that constantly marinating in news can be bad for my peace of mind."

"But don't you think it's important to keep up with what's going on in the world?"

"Yes and no. There is only so much you can do to change the world." He gestured around the kitchen. "For some people, their helplessness in the face of the big picture can lead to despair and misery in what might otherwise be a healthy and productive life. The Amish believe we are *in*, but not *of*, this world. For better or worse, that's the choice we've made to keep our sanity and our faith."

"And for now, that's the only option I have too. It's not like I can watch a little television in the evening."

"As I said, I predict within two or three months you

won't miss it. When I was in the *Englisch* world, I didn't
have the powerful sense of community I have here,
much less my family around me, and religion played
a far less important role in *Englisch* peoples' everyday lives."

"So imagine how much worse it is for those who
don't know what they're missing," said Leah. "The
irony, of course, is I was experiencing that meaning-
lessness without realizing it. I compensated by working.
Some might say by *over*working—" She was interrupted by a chime from the clock in the next room—
five o'clock.

"Yikes, I'd better get going. I told Edith I'd be back
in time for dinner. Or rather, supper." She rose to her
feet and hesitated. "Isaac, I'm sorry I bit your head
off. Please understand I'm learning to cope with the
change in my circumstances. This isn't about you...
it's about me."

"And I probably pushed too hard." He also stood up.
"But thank you for showing me how to better use the
computer program. And if you ever want to write me
something, I won't object."

Walking back to the Bylers' through the late-afternoon
sunshine, she passed a house she had walked by earlier.
A woman in a deep purple dress and black apron hung
laundry on a line while two young children played on
swings hanging from a tree branch. She could hear their
cheerful cries and chatter. The homeyness of the scene
hit Leah in a way she didn't anticipate.

She'd never known siblings. She'd never known a

domestic life, not like what this unknown woman experienced on a daily basis.

The woman looked over and waved at Leah, then continued her task. Leah returned the greeting. Who was happier in her job, she wondered—herself at the height of her fame, or this nameless woman caring for her family's needs and creating a legacy of stability for her children? She had a strong suspicion the answer was obvious.

Lost in thought, she stepped on a branch and winced. She looked down. The branch lay on the side of the road, and it was…crooked.

She stopped and stared as a cold prickle went down her spine. She picked up the stick, about fourteen inches long, full of kinks and warps. She recalled what Isaac had said.

Could her life be described as a straight stick or a crooked one? On the surface, it seemed it wasn't too crooked—she didn't have a string of bad relationships behind her, she'd had a successful career—but was that enough?

Was her life pleasing to God? Before this, she'd never given the matter any thought.

She started walking again, still holding the stick. Her parents had divorced when she was young. Her father had never been in her life. Her mother was now deceased, but she'd raised her daughter to be strong and independent, with an eye toward seeking the fulfillment of a career rather than the chains of domestic life. She had no siblings, no immediate relatives, only a handful of close friends.

Her mother had been so proud of her career in journalism. After her mother's death, Leah had thrown herself even more into her job. For a long time, it had covered the lack of family, friends and community... and now that was gone too.

Now what was left—and what her future might hold—was something she had avoided thinking about.

But she couldn't avoid it forever. Nor could she hide out here among the Amish forever.

Frowning, she tossed the stick aside.

Then she picked it up again and carried it with her.

Chapter Seven

She arrived back at the house in time to see a happy swirl of activity. The children swarmed through the kitchen and living room, the older girls chopped and grated cheese, and Edith spread dough on a circular pan.

"Pizza!" Leah exclaimed. "Not that I'm arguing, but this doesn't strike me as a traditional Amish dish."

"Maybe not, but it sure is tasty." Edith's eyes twinkled. "We easily go through four of them whenever I make it."

Leah slipped upstairs and placed the crooked stick in her dresser drawer. Then she rejoined the family, washed her hands and volunteered for any necessary task. Rachel handed her a lump of mozzarella cheese and a grater.

"Let's see…" Leah looked over the preparation process. "Tomato sauce, homemade. Mozzarella cheese, homemade. Dough for the crust, homemade. Spices, homegrown. Onions, homegrown. Sausage, homemade." She winked at Edith. "This is gonna be much better than anything I could buy frozen at the grocery store."

"Probably." Edith spread sauce on the dough. "I've never had frozen pizza."

"To someone raised on store-bought food, homemade pizza is amazing." She continued grating the cheese, but the journalist in her questioned whether Isaac was right, and even something as ordinary as pizza could be made into an extraordinary article focusing on the homegrown components.

Edith scooped up some of the grated cheese from Leah's pile. "A neighbor showed me how to make pizza a few years ago. It's become a family favorite. Now we have it every Friday night."

"Nothing else going on tonight? No hot dog roasts or anything?"

"Nope. We're not hosting church either, so it will be a quiet weekend for us."

"Hosting church? What do you mean?"

"I'm sorry, I guess you might not know," Edith said as she sprinkled the cheese across the pizzas. "We meet for Sabbath services every other week, not every week. We don't use church buildings. Instead, families rotate to various homes. We hosted a couple months ago, so it will be a while before it's our turn to host again, probably not until well after the *boppli* is born. And since this is our off week, we're not having a church service on Sunday."

"What do you normally do on Sundays when there isn't a church service?"

"It's a day of rest, so we don't do any work except chores that must be done every day, such as milking the cows and feeding the livestock. It's a good time for visiting, or reading or napping. Children will sometimes get together to play games. We'll cook extra food ahead of time, so we don't have to cook. Sundays are lovely days."

"Why don't you have church buildings?"

Edith decorated the pizzas with chopped onions and sausage before answering. "It all goes back to the 1600s. Our ancestors were called the Anabaptists, and they were persecuted all over Europe, so they were forced to meet in secret. They held church services in homes, caves, in the forest—wherever they would be least likely to be discovered. At the time, churches in Europe were huge and very ornate and of course used just once a week. That seemed very wasteful and extravagant. Even after the persecution died down and the Anabaptists were able to meet without fear, they continued to use peoples' homes for services."

"Is that why this house is so spacious?"

"Yes, and I don't know if you've noticed, but many of the walls are like pocket doors. They can be slid back and rooms opened even more, to accommodate all the benches and people."

Leah glanced at the kitchen wall separating it from the living room. Intrigued, she walked over and examined it. "You're right! How clever!"

Edith chuckled. "I love our church services. Oh, and that's another reason we have no church building—we believe church is the people, the body of believers, not any one building or place."

"I've only been here a short time, but already I'm impressed with how unified everyone seems to be."

"*Ja*. We tend to emphasize unity, humility, submission. We feel strongly about maintaining the purity of the body of believers, which is why we prefer to stay apart from the *Englisch* world."

"Isaac mentioned this afternoon how glad he was to be back."

"I'm glad he's back. I just hope he can find a nice girl and settle down soon."

Leah glanced at Edith, but the older woman's head was bent down over her work. "Rachel said much the same thing," she offered in a neutral voice.

"He's doing a good job, caring for his mother."

"Is she widowed?"

"Yes, her husband died a few years ago. He was a good man. It was a hard loss for Eleanor."

"Does Isaac have any brothers or sisters to help out?"

"*Ja*, sure, but they're all married and living on their own. It's tradition for the youngest son to inherit the farm, so Isaac cares for his mother too."

"I noticed she was limping. Do you know why?"

"I think she needs a hip replacement."

This led to a whole new avenue of consideration for Leah, and again her journalistic instincts were piqued. "If she does need an operation, how is that paid for? Do you have insurance?"

"No." Edith slid one of the pizzas into the oven. "Most things we try to treat as we can. For anything more serious, we use doctors and hospitals. It varies by community, but mostly we pay for any health care we need ourselves. But we combine church aid—a sort of tithing—with benefit auctions, and we try to negotiate directly with the hospitals, as well. Most hospitals are very good about working with people who pay cash."

"So if Eleanor needs an operation, everyone pitches in?"

"*Ja*, sure. I mean, how else would it be paid for?"

How indeed? The thought of being without health insurance was a frightening concept for Leah. The care she received after her run-in with the gang members reinforced the need for insurance. But the Amish had figured out a way to do without it, while still taking advantage of medical care when needed. "Impressive," she murmured.

"Not really." Edith pushed in another pizza. "It's just a matter of shared responsibility. Medical needs go beyond us as individuals. They're shared concerns, church concerns. We don't want the government to pay for our things. We think we should take care of our own members."

"That's why your barn raisings are so famous."

"Perhaps. But we don't want to be famous. We just want to mind our own business."

Pride again. Or rather, an aversion to it. But it was this sense of community that Leah found both baffling…and exciting.

"It's funny," she mused. "I don't think I ever realized I was lonely before. But I think I was. I don't think you, or anyone else I've met here, suffer from loneliness."

Edith looked at her with surprise. "Of course not!"

While the pizzas were cooking, the daughters of the family tidied the kitchen and set the table. Sarah brought laundry in, already folded, in a basket. Eliza fetched in several gallons of milk from the barn, where Ivan and the two older boys were milking the cows. Even the youngest boy "helped" by re-folding the already-folded dishtowels in a kitchen drawer. Rachel skimmed cream from yesterday's milk and put the rest of the skimmed milk away to make cheese later, she told Leah. "Probably more mozzarella, since we like it on pizzas."

Leah felt more and more helpless in the face of the family's constant—and seemingly effortless—industry.

"There's so much I don't know how to do," she finally blurted. "And I don't know how I can help without being more of a hindrance."

Sarah chuckled. "Here. You can cut the pizzas." She pulled one out of the oven and slid it onto some large towels laid on the counter. Then she handed Leah a rotary cutter.

Ivan and the boys sidled in and washed up just as she finished cutting up the pizzas. "I love pizza!" announced the oldest boy with a grin.

Leah smiled at him. She hadn't spent a lot of time around children before, but the Byler kids were terrific.

Seated, the family bowed their heads for silent prayer, then reached for slices of their favorites and began eating.

"So what did you do with Isaac?" Ivan spoke with his mouth full.

Besides argue? she thought. "He was having trouble understanding how to do some things on one of his computer programs," she replied. "I showed him how to do it."

"It's nice to see his magazine grow." Edith patted her stomach. "Though not as fast as this little one! But I've heard it's being stocked in lots of *Englisch* stores."

"You'd be surprised how many English have an interest in rural life," agreed Leah. "I think if you're trapped in a city, it's only normal to want birdsong and stars at night."

"Well, it's more than just chirping birds and happy rainbows." Rachel spoke with the first hint of sarcasm Leah had heard. "Folks have to understand it's hard work. It's just work we prefer."

"That's why I said this morning you'll work off any food you eat," added Edith. "We're busy all the time. Most of us like it that way."

"But you're busy on your own schedules, doing whatever needs doing rather than working by anyone else's schedule, such as working for a boss. I kind of like that idea."

Ivan shrugged. "You get used to it."

When supper was over, Edith told her brood, "Prayers in half an hour. Make sure you have your chores done."

"Prayers?" Leah had a sinking feeling inside.

"Ivan leads us in Bible readings every night." A concerned look spread over the older woman's face. "But it's in German. I hope you can follow." Her face brightened. "But we have an English Bible. You can use that if it's too hard to listen in German."

Leah could hardly beg off attending the nightly ritual—the Bylers were being too kind to her—and if she was going to be part of this community for the next few months, she had to sit through whatever was thrown at her, including Bible readings.

It was almost dusk by the time the chores were finished and the family gathered in the spacious living room. The children sat on various articles of furniture, quiet and expectant. Edith pulled a book off a book-shelf. "Ivan, what verses?"

"I think from Hebrews, first chapter," he replied. He lit an oil lamp on the small table next to him and pulled the large volume into his lap.

"Just follow as best you can." Edith handed Leah a soft leather English Bible, worn with age.

Leah didn't have the heart to tell the motherly woman she didn't have the faintest clue how to find Hebrews, whether in German or in English. So that was another task she must set herself to learn—what books were found where in the Bible, so she could at least pretend to follow along.

"Nachdem vorzeiten Gott manchmal und mancher-leiweise geredet hat zu den Vätern durch die Proph-eten," began Ivan in a clear, melodious voice. Leah frantically tried to translate in her mind.

It was hopeless. Ivan read at an easy pace, but Leah's fluency in German was not up to following the ancient, beautiful words. So she just sat, mesmerized by the majesty and cadence of the language.

She found herself watching the children. Ranging in age as they were from four to twenty, they all sat and listened attentively. How many *Englisch* children would be as quiet and focused while listening to a Bible chapter? What magic did the Amish use to raise such respectful kids? Again the journalist in her was piqued.

With a jolt, she realized what Isaac said earlier might be true—she might be staring at a whole new career. How many people wanted to know the answers to the questions forming in her mind?

She'd spent her career dealing with cutting-edge

news that often dealt with the ugly, seamier side of life—"If it bleeds, it leads." But untold millions of people quietly went about their business in ways that weren't often profiled. Small triumphs such as doing laundry without electricity or having six children listen attentively to their father read the Bible—surely this would interest people who wanted to raise good kids or lighten their carbon footprint?

She had been so busy building her career as an investigative journalist that she had never thought about alternatives.

"Amein," said Ivan, and closed the Bible.

"Danke, Daed." Sarah rose and stretched. The other children got up, as well.

"That was beautiful," said Leah, "though I couldn't follow most of it."

"Not even in the English Bible?" inquired Edith.

Leah didn't admit she couldn't locate the right spot. "Do you mind if I take this up to my room and read it in the evening?" she asked instead. "It would be easier to follow in English."

"Ja, sure. Consider it yours, in fact."

"Thank you." Leah felt touched.

The Bylers lit a couple more lamps and settled down to quiet pursuits. "I think some popcorn, *ja*?" suggested Edith, and the children agreed.

The mother departed for the kitchen, and Leah heard sounds from the darkened room lit only by the lamp Edith carried with her. In a few minutes she heard a pop, then several, then a blizzard as the corn exploded. After the sound died down, Edith brought in an enormous bowl of popcorn along with several smaller bowls so they could all help themselves.

Filling their bowls, the younger children sprawled on the floor playing a game called Aggravation on a wooden board. The older children read. Edith took out a knitting basket. Ivan perused his Bible. In the midst of such quiet pursuits, Leah sat near Sarah and shared the light from a lamp. She opened the Bible she carried and read bits here and there. The popcorn, made with homemade butter, melted in her mouth.

These, too, were new experiences for her. The house was quiet except for the chatter of the children at their game and the sound of crunching popcorn. No music played, no television blared, no video games rocked the room. Instead she heard crickets through the open windows and saw fireflies flashing over the darkened fields. Once in a while Ivan made a comment to his wife about something he read, or Edith made a remark of her own.

This, she thought, was how every home in America must have been before radios were invented. Quiet was the norm. Conversation was the norm. Reading was the norm. Could this be something to write about? If not, it might be useful to simply record her thoughts and impressions and experiences.

"I wonder," she dared venture, "if you have some paper and a pen I could use?"

"*Ja*, of course." Rachel rose and reached for the materials on a nearby shelf and even supplied a clipboard.

"Thank you." That's another thing she'd have to get used to—writing by hand instead of on a computer.

She started by writing down what she remembered

about doing laundry by hand. Once in a while she asked a question of Sarah—"What other kinds of ways did you do laundry before you had your current machine?" or "How do you make laundry detergent?" which sparked a spirited discussion among the women of the family.

How she longed to photograph the cozy family scene. Instead, she took a fresh sheet of paper and painted a verbal picture, writing down descriptions of the children, the games, the lamps, the chatter, the popcorn, the crickets.

How deprived her own childhood seemed by comparison. Not just because of her parents' divorce and then death; but her own adult life, solitary and alone in her apartment, except for when she worked late.

"This is so nice," she finally said aloud.

"What is?" asked Edith.

"Just the family, all together in this room. You have no idea how rare this is in the wider world."

Ivan chuckled and closed his Bible. "What do the *Englisch* do in the evenings?"

"Watch television or play games on a computer. It seems not many people talk much anymore. Kids—" she gestured toward the children on the floor "—are either playing computer games or in their rooms. Gathering together as a family is…" She groped for the right word. "Special."

Sarah wrinkled her nose. "This is why I came back after my *rumspringa*. I like being with my family."

"You'll have a whole new family next November," teased Rachel.

"*Ja*, perhaps." A blush stained her cheeks. "But we won't be far away."

"How far away is Aaron's farm?" asked Leah.

Sarah gestured. "Only about a quarter mile in that direction. His property and our property are side by side."

"You seem so sure," murmured Leah.

Sarah looked puzzled. "Sure of what?"

"Sure that Aaron is the right man for you."

"Of course he is. How could he not be?"

"But you're so young!"

Edith interrupted. "Not really. And you have to understand—young people among the Amish already know they're compatible in the critical areas of faith, family and finances. After that, it's just a matter of finding someone who—how do the *Englisch* put it?—lights your fire." She winked at Ivan.

Leah laughed at the blatant flirtation. "I guess that just hasn't happened to me yet."

"It's also why Isaac hasn't gotten married yet," said Rachel. Leah thought she saw a gleam of mischief in the young woman's eyes as she introduced the subject. "He's just different enough that most women have their doubts about him."

"And he's a bit older than most men when they get married," added Sarah.

"But he's a good man," Ivan said, as he chewed some popcorn. "Works hard. Takes care of his mother. Helps whenever he's needed. He's an asset to the community."

"Even if he's doing stuff on a computer?" asked Leah.

"Even so. But he didn't start the magazine without first seeking permission from the bishop and the elders. He knows—none better—the problems computers can cause with the *Englisch* world. The ones you just talked about. He's using it just for business, and using it so it doesn't affect the community, which is why the bishop gave him permission."

"This bishop—does his approval have to be sought for anything like that?"

"Bishops carry a heavy responsibility," said Ivan. "They're charged with maintaining traditions and behaviors that benefit the community, not the individual. If something is introduced that would be disruptive, a bishop won't approve." He took another handful of popcorn. "Any new technology we've introduced must be shown to be beneficial, such as generators to run the milking machines for dairies. If a dairy farmer loses his livelihood because he can't compete with an *Englisch* dairy, then that's a big loss and a detriment to the community. But it doesn't mean the dairyman can light his home with his generator, or use it for frivolous purposes—just for milking his animals."

Leah tapped her pen on the paper. "I think I'm beginning to see why it's such a rare thing for Isaac to be using a computer."

"Ja." Ivan licked the butter off his fingers. "And he hasn't abused it. It hasn't affected the community in a bad way, and so far everyone likes the magazine."

Edith yawned and glanced at the clock. "It's late. This one should have been in bed already." She put down her knitting and reached for her youngest son, whose head was nodding. "Tomorrow is a busy day."

"Ja." Sarah grinned at Leah. "You should see what we have in store for you tomorrow!"

"Like what?" Leah tried not to panic.

"You'll see!" crowed Eliza, getting into the spirit.

Edith chuckled. "Don't let them worry you. We won't work you too hard."

"But we won't let you sleep in either," said Sarah. "Up with the roosters!"

Leah felt herself flush. "I don't normally sleep that late."

"You'll get into the routine soon enough." Edith gathered up her son. The family filed out and washed up in the bathroom or at the kitchen sink.

Leah made sure to fetch the Bible before heading upstairs to bed. She had a chapter or two in Hebrews to locate and read.

Chapter Eight

A rooster crowing right below her window jerked Leah out of a sound sleep. The eastern horizon glowed with a bright light, but the rest of the sky was still flushed dark. What time was it?

She yawned and stretched. Whatever the time, she heard distant activity downstairs, so evidently she wasn't the first one awake.

Feeling virtuous for being an early riser, she dressed and padded down the stairs in her bare feet. She found Edith and Sarah in the kitchen, chatting softly in *Deitsch*. "Good morning."

Both women turned. "Good morning!" they replied in unison. "You're up early today," added Sarah.

"I had a rooster alarm clock. Can I help with something?" Whether or not she was taught that domestic chores were oppressive, she was still a guest and felt compelled to ask.

Sarah rolled and cut biscuits. "Do you want to make gravy? We're having biscuits and gravy for breakfast."

Leah bit her lip. "What do I do?"

Over the wood cookstove, Sarah showed Leah how to mix butter and flour together, then dribble in milk until the mixture thickened. "Now add just a bit of thyme," said Sarah, reaching for a jar on a shelf. "Then we can flavor it either with crumbled sausage, or with bits of bacon. Which do you prefer?"

"How about sausage?"

"Then you can chop it up, as well. Here, put the pot on this side of the stove where it's not so hot. If you come with me, I'll show you where we store our meat."

Lighting an oil lamp, Sarah led the way into the basement to the amazing shelves of canned food. "We keep the meat over here," said Sarah. "See the labels on the shelves? Here's sausage." She picked up a jar that held what looked like crumbled pork meat inside.

"You canned this yourself?"

"Yes. See the date on the lid? That was from one of our pigs last year."

Leah shook her head. "Your skills and creativity amaze me. I wondered how you kept meat from going bad without refrigerators or freezers."

"We freeze some in the winter, but whatever's not eaten by spring, we can it so it stays preserved. No sense wasting *Gott*'s bounty by letting food go bad."

Holding the pint jar of sausage, Leah followed Sarah back up the stairs to the kitchen. She found the other daughters awake, sipping tea and helping with breakfast. Rachel dipped something out of a large glass jar.

"What's that?" asked Leah, placing the sausage on the counter.

"Cream," the young woman replied. "This is yesterday's milk. *Daed* will be in shortly with this morning's milk."

"Here's how to open a canning jar," said Sarah, handing Leah a small implement. "You pry the lid off, and we keep the lid and gasket. These canning lids and gaskets are reusable."

Following instructions, Leah scooped the sausage out of the jar, chopped it fine and added it to the gravy. Despite feeling like she was all thumbs, she found it pleasant to work in a kitchen full of women, chatting in English for her sake and engaged in creating a hearty meal out of home-produced ingredients.

By the time the sun peeked over the horizon, Ivan clattered into the kitchen. *"Guder mariye, guder mariye,"* he called, shouldering open the door since his hands were clutching two brimful buckets of milk. "Ah, Leah, you're up early."

"Yes, I decided not to be lazy anymore," she bantered, relieving him of one of the buckets while he hefted the other one on top the kitchen counter.

The three boys came stumbling into the kitchen, yawning and rubbing their eyes. The youngest went straight to his mother, who lifted him and sat down in a kitchen chair with him on her lap, snuggling in what was clearly a morning routine.

Ivan poured himself a cup of coffee and added some of the cream Rachel had just skimmed, along with a scant teaspoon of honey. "Have you had coffee?" he asked Leah.

"I prefer tea, actually."

"Oh, we have tea." Rachel reached for a jar of loose-leaf blend. She prepared a mug for her. "Tomorrow morning, help yourself. We keep it here, and the tea strainers are in this drawer."

With the entire family up, the girls set the table while Edith strained the milk and poured it into clean jars, which she capped. "Those will go down into the cellar after breakfast," she explained to Leah. "Tomorrow we'll skim the cream. Normally we'd make butter, too, but since tomorrow is the Sabbath, we'll wait until Monday."

"Sit yourself down, boys," Ivan told his sons.

Leah seated herself as well, as Edith settled the youngest into a booster seat. Everyone bowed their heads for a silent prayer.

Including Leah. Almost without realizing it, she found herself being grateful for the food upon the table. It was gratifying to know she had helped prepare some of it.

Ivan started with the scrambled eggs, dumping some onto his plate, then adding some to his youngest son's. "Even though I still have a lot of work to do to finish those pieces for the Cleveland store, I'm going to walk the pasture fences and tighten a few spots today. Boys, you can help me find where Matilda—that's one of our Jersey cows," he added to Leah, "keeps pushing over the fence into the horse pasture."

"What's on the agenda today?" Leah asked Edith.

"Laundry." Edith counted off on her fingers. "Housecleaning. Weeding. Picking strawberries. Baking. Tomorrow is the Sabbath, so we'll all take baths tonight. Rachel, I'll ask you to make some cheese today," continued Edith, eyeing the gallon jars of milk on the counter.

"We'll strip the beds and wash sheets today too. Lots to do!" She chuckled.

Throughout the day, Leah got a crash course in laundry, dishes, cooking, picking strawberries, canning preserves, and making bread. Mouth agape, she watched as Rachel made mozzarella cheese out of yesterday's milk. The house was cleaned from top to bottom and the bed sheets washed.

By late afternoon, Leah found herself gathering dried laundry with Eliza, the youngest daughter.

"It looks pretty, don't you think?" she asked Eliza, pointing to the white sheets moving in the breeze.

"Ja," agreed Eliza. "And I like having nice clean sheets on my bed."

But even this simple task required some explanation from the twelve-year-old. "You might want to fold them as you go," instructed Eliza. She showed Leah how to unpin one corner of each sheet and gather it across the length until the last pin came off. "That saves a lot of folding in the end."

Leah gave a huff of annoyance at herself. "You're, what, sixteen years younger than me—and you know a lot more than I do."

Eliza looked at the ground for a moment. "It's just practice," she mumbled.

"And I need a lot more practice."

"But why?" asked Eliza, reaching for another sheet. "You won't be here too long, will you?"

"I don't know." Leah placed a folded sheet in the basket. "I don't know how long I'll be here."

"Could you stay if you wanted?"

"I—I don't know. Your parents are being so kind to me… I certainly couldn't stay with them forever."

"You should marry Isaac," pronounced Eliza with the assurance of youth.

Leah felt her cheeks flare. "Why do you say that?"

"Because he's already courting you. He's a good man."

"Does *everyone* think he's courting me?"

"*Ja*, probably."

Her lips thinned. So this was how rumors started. "Well, he's not," she snapped. Seeing the girl's stricken expression, she softened. "I'm sorry. It's just that Isaac can't court me. He rubs me the wrong way. Plus he only just met me, and I'm not Amish."

"Maybe you could be."

Her curiosity got the better of her. "How does someone become Amish?"

Eliza looked puzzled. "I don't know. Maybe talk to the bishop? He'd know."

"The next question is—would I want to?" She didn't really mean for the words to be spoken out loud, but they were.

Eliza unpinned another sheet. "I like it here. I don't know if I want to go anywhere else for my *rumspringa*. It sounds dangerous out there. Like the man who hurt your face."

"It *can* be dangerous." Leah sighed. Eliza was still blessed with the innocence of youth. "But there's a lot of good too."

"There's a lot of good *here*."

"I can see that." She glanced around at the tidy farm, better understanding now the sheer hard work it entailed. "I don't know if I'm ready to give up modern conveniences and learn to do everything by hand."

"I like working with my hands. I like doing useful things."

Leah found herself being schooled by this preteen and wasn't sure she was happy about it. She came from a world where labor was avoided by the use of laborsaving devices. Yet there's no question the work the Bylers did on a daily basis accomplished useful things. It produced cheese. And strawberry preserves. And furniture.

With a start, Leah realized what the Bylers had that she lacked: peace of mind. It wasn't just the bucolic rural setting either. It was the assurance that work was the answer, that trust in God was the source, that unity was strength.

The young girl was right. There was a lot of good here.

"Eliza!" called Edith from the porch. "There is some food I want you to bring to Anna Yoder."

"Ja, Mamm," replied Eliza. "We're almost finished."

Leah dropped her last folded sheet into the basket, then took one handle as Eliza took the other and helped carry it toward the porch.

Inside, the kitchen was cooler and cleaner than she'd left it, with the older girls tidying. "Put those away," Edith told her youngest daughter, "and I'll have something ready for you to take."

"Who is Anna Yoder?" asked Leah.

"A widow in poor health." Edith paused to hold her stomach and close her eyes. Leah suspected the baby was kicking. "She lives with her son and his wife, but I

"4 for 4" MINI-SURVEY

We are prepared to **REWARD** you with 4 FREE Books and Free Gifts for completing our MINI SURVEY!

Romance

Suspense

You'll get up to...

4 FREE BOOKS & FREE GIFTS

just for participating in our Mini Survey!

Get Up To 4 Free Books!

Dear Reader,

IT'S A FACT: if you answer 4 quick questions, we'll send you 4 FREE REWARDS from each series you try!

Try **Love Inspired® Romance Larger-Print** books and fall in love with inspirational romances that take you on an uplifting journey of faith, forgiveness and hope.

Try **Love Inspired® Suspense Larger-Print** books where courage and optimism unite in stories of faith and love in the face of danger.

Or **TRY BOTH!**

I'm not kidding you. As a leading publisher of women's fiction, we value your opinions... and your time. That's why we are prepared to reward you handsomely for completing our mini-survey. In fact, we have 4 Free Rewards for you, including 2 free books and 2 free gifts from each series you try!

Thank you for participating in our survey,

Pam Powers

www.ReaderService.com

To get your 4 FREE REWARDS:
Complete the survey below and return the insert today to receive up to 4 FREE BOOKS and FREE GIFTS guaranteed!

"4 for 4" MINI-SURVEY

1 Is reading one of your favorite hobbies?

☐ YES ☐ NO

2 Do you prefer to read instead of watch TV?

☐ YES ☐ NO

3 Do you read newspapers and magazines?

☐ YES ☐ NO

4 Do you enjoy trying new book series with FREE BOOKS?

☐ YES ☐ NO

Please send me my Free Rewards, consisting of **2 Free Books from each series I select** and **Free Mystery Gifts**. I understand that I am under no obligation to buy anything, as explained on the back of this card.

☐ **Love Inspired® Romance Larger-Print** (122/322 IDL GQ5X)
☐ **Love Inspired® Suspense Larger-Print** (107/307 IDL GQ5X)
☐ **Try Both** (122/322 & 107/307 IDL GQ6A)

FIRST NAME	LAST NAME

ADDRESS

APT.#	CITY

STATE/PROV.	ZIP/POSTAL CODE

EMAIL ☐ Please check this box if you would like to receive newsletters and promotional emails from Harlequin Enterprises ULC and its affiliates. You can unsubscribe anytime.

LI/SLI-520-MS20

HARLEQUIN READER SERVICE—Here's how it works:

Accepting your 2 free books and 2 free gifts (gifts valued at approximately $10.00 retail) places you under no obligation to buy anything. You may keep the books and gifts and return the shipping statement marked "cancel." If you do not cancel, approximately one month later we'll send you 6 more books from each series you have chosen, and bill you at our low, subscribers-only discount price. Love Inspired® Romance Larger-Print books and Love Inspired® Suspense Larger-Print books consist of 6 books each month and cost just $5.99 each in the U.S. or $6.24 each in Canada. That is a savings of at least 17% off the cover price. It's quite a bargain! Shipping and handling is just 50¢ per book in the U.S. and $1.25 per book in Canada*. You may return any shipment at our expense and cancel at any time — or you may continue to receive monthly shipments at our low, subscribers-only discount price plus shipping and handling. *Terms and prices subject to change without notice. Prices do not include sales taxes which will be charged (if applicable) based on your state or country of residence. Canadian residents will be charged applicable taxes. Offer not valid in Quebec. Books received may not be as shown. All orders subject to approval. Credit or debit balances in a customer's account(s) may be offset by any other outstanding balance owed by or to the customer. Please allow 3 to 4 weeks for delivery. Offer available while quantities last.

▲ If offer card is missing write to: Harlequin Reader Service, P.O. Box 1341, Buffalo, NY 14240-8531 or visit www.ReaderService.com ▲

BUSINESS REPLY MAIL
FIRST-CLASS MAIL   PERMIT NO. 717   BUFFALO, NY

POSTAGE WILL BE PAID BY ADDRESSEE

HARLEQUIN READER SERVICE
PO BOX 1341
BUFFALO NY 14240-8571

NO POSTAGE
NECESSARY
IF MAILED
IN THE
UNITED STATES

have my doubts about the young wife's cooking. I like to help out when I can."

"It's constant, isn't it?"

"What's constant?"

"The…the sense of community. Everyone thinking about everyone else."

"*Ja*, sure. How else could it be?"

Leah didn't have the heart to tell the older woman she didn't even know who lived in the apartment next door to her in LA. Asking for help from those unknown residents was out of the question. Nor would her neighbors ask her for help. It was a much different world here.

After Eliza left with a basket packed with goodies, Edith dropped into a kitchen chair. "Ooh," she grunted. "This little one is getting heavy."

"Are you okay?" Having never spent any time around pregnant women, Leah wondered if Edith was ill.

"*Ja*, fine. I just get tired more easily. That's another reason I look forward to the Sabbath—I can take a nap without guilt."

"Can I get you something? Some tea, perhaps?"

The older woman smiled. "*Ja*, *danke*, that would be nice."

Leah felt proud she was becoming comfortable enough in the kitchen that she knew how to prepare a mug without bothering Sarah or Rachel, who continued to clean up.

She set the cup of hot tea on the table, along with a jar of honey. "Thank you." Edith spooned in a scant half teaspoon of sweetener and stirred. She sipped. "How are you settling in, do you think?"

"I think I'm bothering Sarah and Rachel far more than I should." Leah smiled at the two young women.

"How is it you never developed skills needed for cooking and such?"

"Simple. I blame modern conveniences."

"Didn't your mother ever teach you how to sew or cook?"

Leah looked down at her hands. "My mother and father divorced when I was very young. I rarely saw my father. Mom raised me by herself and was always working, trying to make a living, so she simply didn't have the time to pass on any domestic skills she might have possessed."

"Oh, I'm so sorry…"

Leah looked up to see deep sympathy in Edith's blue eyes. "Mom's wish was always that I would have a better life than she was able to give me. That's why she put such a high value on a career."

"How is your mom doing now?"

"She died in a car crash when I was nineteen."

"Oh no! Are you all alone? No family nearby?"

"None. I was an only child, and so were both my parents. I have no extended family."

Leah thought Edith might burst into tears at this news, her face looked so stricken. Even Sarah and Rachel suspended their work, staring at her wide-eyed.

"Hey, it's not as bad as all that," she said into the silence. "I did okay. I had a nice career and a nice apartment."

"But no support structure, no people around you who love you." Edith swallowed hard. "And then your career was taken away too."

"Yeah, I didn't see that one coming." Leah traced a shape on the table with a fingernail. "That's why I feel so at loose ends. I don't know quite what to do with myself, and I'm so grateful you're offering me a place for the moment."

"Have you asked *Gott* for help?" inquired Edith with the tone of someone for whom this was a normal part of everyday life.

"Um, no." Leah felt awkward saying that out loud. "I'm still busy trying not to be mad at Him for this." She touched the scar on her cheek.

"Och, things happen for a reason. Your job now is to figure out what the reason is."

Leah didn't dare confess the depth of her lack of faith to this kindly woman. "I'm sure you're right," she said evasively.

With a clatter, Ivan came into the kitchen followed by his two older sons. "Time for milking," he announced. "Sarah, are the buckets clean?"

"*Ja*, there." The older daughter pointed.

"Back to work, then," said Edith, hauling her ever-growing form out of the chair. "Girls, let's get water heating. Everyone needs a bath tonight. There you are," she added to her youngest child, who came stumbling into the kitchen rubbing his eyes. He clearly had just woken up from a nap. Edith scooped him up and said something softly in *Deitsch*.

"How do you take baths?" inquired Leah. She had a special interest in the answer to this question.

"In the bathtub, of course. But since we don't have running water, we use a bucket system."

The brief moment of rest was over. Leah thought it was no wonder Edith looked forward to the Sabbath as a chance to cease the unremitting toil of running a large household without the aid of electric appliances.

Within half an hour, Ivan returned with buckets

brimming with milk. Rachel started straining the milk, and Sarah scalded the buckets clean. Eliza returned from her errand, and Leah helped her set the table. Edith stirred a pot on the stove and put hot food in serving dishes. The boys washed their hands at the sink. Then the family sat down, bowed their heads in silent prayer and started eating.

"Aah, the Sabbath," said Ivan with his mouth full. "It will be nice to rest."

"Many *Englisch* people work on Sundays," observed Leah, thinking of how many weekends she had worked.

Eliza looked shocked. "But the Fourth Commandment!" she blurted.

Edith made a shushing gesture. "Not everyone lives by the Good Book, *dochder*," she said.

"It's true." Leah pushed some food around on her plate. "But I'm starting to see how a society works when people *do* follow the Good Book."

"*Ja*, it's nice to have an instruction manual," agreed Ivan. "We don't have to—what's the term?—reinvent the wheel when it comes to living our lives."

"But you do, kind of," contradicted Leah. "Because the outside world moves so fast, the Amish have to adjust, too, deciding what technology to reject."

"That's true," agreed Ivan. "But it's an effortless process. Mostly. Once in a while a thorny dilemma comes up, such as Isaac wanting to use a computer, but when it comes to such things as using machinery to power woodworking tools or dairy equipment—well, such decisions come down from the bishop and the elders, and we don't have to question it."

Leah wondered if that chain of command made the

Bylers uneasy or content. She guessed the latter. They didn't have angst about whether their limited technology damaged their most important criteria in life— community ties and devotion to God.

There was no Bible reading that night, as it was past the younger children's bedtime by the time everyone was clean.

But as Leah lay in bed, on fresh sheets, she realized how tired she was and yet—oddly—exhilarated. She had *done* things today. She had picked strawberries, helped make preserves and assisted with any number of tasks the Byler family routinely undertook.

It had been, she thought with a small shock, a long time since she'd felt satisfaction at a day's work, and she wondered if it was a heresy of some sort to feel the emotion in conjunction with domestic chores. What would her mother think?

This train of thought led to another. She recalled Edith's words earlier: "Have you asked *Gott* for help? Things happen for a reason. Your job now is to figure out what the reason is."

What could possibly be the reason behind losing a career and gaining a facial disfigurement? It made no sense.

But the fact remained—she didn't know what her future held. Mentally she shrugged. Maybe she *should* pray. What did she have to lose?

"God," she whispered, feeling rather foolish, "I don't understand why You did this, but it's done. Please show me what direction I should go."

Then she fell asleep.

Chapter Nine

She woke early and felt the same sense of urgency to get dressed and downstairs as before. But this time she found only Rachel in the kitchen, sipping tea and reading a Bible at the kitchen table. Her hair was in a loose braid down her back and she didn't have her *kapp* on.

"Guder mariye," Leah said, pleased to say it in *Deitsch*.

Rachel raised her head and smiled. *"Guder mariye."*

"I thought the rest of the family would be up by now."

"It's the Sabbath, and we have no church service today. They're sleeping in."

Leah chuckled and shoved a pin back into her bun, readjusting her *kapp*. "And I thought I was being so good and virtuous, getting up early."

"I'm an early bird anyway, and it's a good time for me to read Scripture without everyone around me."

"And I've interrupted." Leah felt awkward. "I'm so sorry…"

"No, don't apologize. I'm just finished." As if to

prove it, Rachel closed the large volume. "Make yourself some tea. The water's hot."

Leah scooped tea leaves into a strainer, poured hot water, added a touch of milk and honey, and sat at the table. "So it's a day of relaxing?"

"Don't you feel you need it?"

"Oh yeah," she replied with such feeling that Rachel laughed.

"It's why *Gott* provided it for us. It gives us a chance to…" Rachel's eyes glinted with mischief. "Recharge our batteries."

"No cooking today?"

"Not really. We prepared a lot of extra food yesterday, so we just eat leftovers. I expect we'll have some visitors later on—Aaron for sure, and probably Isaac, if I don't miss my guess."

"Isaac." Leah looked down at her tea. "So, should I discourage him from visiting? From seeing me?"

"I don't know. How do you feel about him?"

"Does it matter? I'm not Amish."

"I suppose you're right." Rachel rubbed her chin. "If things get more serious, I guess he'll have to lay the matter before the bishop."

"Whoa! What do you mean by serious?"

"Isn't it obvious?"

"You mean marriage?" She stared at Rachel, feeling prickles of panic down her scalp. "Rachel, I've only met the man a couple days ago. We don't share a faith, which is so important to him. He can't be thinking of marriage so soon!"

The younger woman shrugged. "Sure he can. And he obviously is."

"He doesn't know me! And I don't know him!"

"Well, that's why he visits. So he—and you—can remedy that."

"But why would he focus on me, of all people?"

"I suspect it's because you're *Englisch* and understand a lot of what he experienced when he was out in the world. But if he marries you, he'll have to leave. So that's a problem. Or you could become Amish."

The clunk of footsteps interrupted their conversation as Ivan came into the kitchen, yawning. "Morning." He rubbed his eyes. "I'd best go milk before the ladies explode." He bustled about, grabbing clean buckets, and disappeared out the back door.

"I didn't mean to distress you," resumed Rachel. She reached out and touched Leah's hand, wrapped around the mug. "*Gott* will lead you. Just follow Him. But don't shut Isaac out—he's been through a lot, and acceptance into the community is important to him."

Others came into the kitchen at that moment, and in the bustle of greetings and hot drinks, more intimate conversation was impossible.

The tenor of the house was more relaxed as the morning went on. Except for vital chores, no one worked. The children played, the adults relaxed and read books out on the porch, and Aaron did indeed come by to visit with his betrothed.

And in the back of her mind, Leah wondered if— and when—Isaac would come by.

It was almost with a sense of relief that she saw him coming down the road. It gave her time to compose herself, to summon up some of the innate calmness she admired in Rachel.

"Guder nammidaag, Isaac," called Sarah from the porch swing where she sat next to Aaron.

"Guder nammidaag." He paused, one foot on the lower porch step, and asked Aaron about his corn crop.

Leah lingered in the kitchen, feeling self-conscious. But when he finally knocked on the screen door and she called "Come in!" he hardly gave her time to think about it.

"Would you care to walk to the pond?" he inquired.

"What pond?"

"There's a pretty pond about half a mile that way." He pointed. "Right off the road. It belongs to the Millers, but they're generous about letting people walk around it."

What else could she say? "Sure."

Moments later she found herself striding next to him along the road. Her feet had toughened up a bit, so she wasn't walking as slowly as before.

But her mind was in turmoil, and she knew the only way to calm herself was to face the problem head-on.

"Isaac, Rachel said something rather disturbing the other day."

"Ja?"

"Yes. She said you're acting like a courting man."

Silence. Leah sneaked a peek sideways. He stared straight ahead, his curly hair springing from under the straw hat.

"Maybe I am," he said at last.

The air whooshed out of Leah's lungs. "Isaac, you know that's impossible. I'm just a visitor, I'm not Amish and we've only known each other a few days."

"I know. Believe me, I *know*."

"Then why me?"

"I don't know. There's something about you." He glanced at her, then resumed his straightforward gaze. "You're the only one who can understand the context of my experiences in the wider world. You're the only one who's seen *Jurassic Park*. You're the only one who understands something of what goes into making a magazine. You're easy to talk to. And you're pretty."

She was so startled at his last words that she stopped dead in her tracks. "You're kidding."

He stopped and looked at her. A smile quirked the corners of his mouth. "Why does that surprise you?"

"Because I'm not." The words were blunt, bitter.

"If you're referring to the scar, I beg to differ. It doesn't change the way you look, not after the first few seconds. Then no one sees it."

She wanted to believe him. She wanted desperately to believe him, to believe she could recapture something of the appearance that made her the darling of the news camera.

"I used to be beautiful, you know," she said low. Even as she uttered the words, she recognized how shallow they sounded.

"You still are," he replied. "But I should hope you'd know it's not a huge factor with us. Perhaps it comes across as a cliché, but we still see the inside of people, not the outside. I think that's why we discourage photographs of people. They put too much emphasis on individuality. We prefer to see and think about people for other things besides their outward physical appearance."

She sighed. Next to Rachel's stoic acceptance of her

own physical challenges, Leah's obsession with her face seemed heartless and small. She started walking again.

"Penny for your thoughts?" Isaac paced alongside her.

"Just thinking what a shallow person I am, worrying about how I look." She stared straight ahead. "Especially in light of Rachel's fortitude with her condition."

"Rachel's pretty special," he agreed. "She has more strength than almost anyone I've ever met."

"Changing the subject… Can I ask you a personal question?"

"Of course."

"Every Amish man I've met so far has a beard. No mustache, but a beard. Why don't you?"

He stroked his chin. "Because by tradition only married men wear beards. I'm not married. Yet," he added.

That made Leah's face grow warm. His meaning was clear. "Oh. I see."

"Here's the pond," he said.

It was a pretty little body of water, right at the edge of the road, ringed by trees. In the warm June sunshine, it offered a cool and shady respite.

Without asking, he led the way toward a willow and sat down beneath it, inches from the water. Leah followed.

"Did you figure out those issues with the computer program?" Leah was anxious to table the whole courtship thing.

"Yes. I messed up a couple of times but finally got it. If it wasn't for the awful typing, I could have gotten a whole section transcribed. I *hate* typing."

"Really? I love it. I clocked myself once and hit one hundred twenty-five words per minute."

He stared at her. "You're kidding."

"Of course not. Why, what's the matter? It's nothing unusual."

He scrubbed a hand over his face. "Unless you didn't learn to type until you were an adult. Can I hire you to help me prepare the next issue?"

"Seriously?"

"Yes, of course."

Her mind churned. It was clear he wanted her help, and it was obvious this was one thing she could do well, but she also knew she wouldn't feel comfortable getting paid.

"We'll talk about it when the time comes," she prevaricated. She wrapped her arms around her updrawn knees and stared out across the still waters of the pond. A turtle blinked at her from a sunny perch on a half-submerged log. "It might help me feel more useful here," she admitted at last. "I'm only just learning the domestic skills the Byler girls can do in their sleep. I'm still all thumbs."

"I think," he offered, "you might find you'll enjoy the kinds of information I put in the magazine. It occurs to me news journalism usually means covering unpleasant things—death and mayhem, natural disasters and car crashes. *This* is negative, *that* is negative. But with the magazine, I cover positive things—the businesses people have created, the techniques they've mastered to do a difficult task, how they solve problems."

"Yes!" Leah sat up straighter. "Do you know what

Rachel *did* yesterday? She made cheese! And I watched her!"

"And you found that amazing?"

"Of course! She started with milk and ended with something completely different. I've never seen anything like it."

"My mother makes cheese too. Most women do. It's the best way to use up extra milk."

Leah shook her head. "I find myself very intimidated by Sarah and Rachel. Even Eliza. There's so much they know how to do."

He grinned. "This is good. You're starting to come alive again. I detected a certain degree of apathy and deadness of spirit at first, but you're a fighter and you're starting to pull out."

Leah fingered her scar before she realized what she was doing, then snatched her hand away. "Maybe," she muttered.

"Look." He laid a hand on hers for a moment, then withdrew it. "I know losing your career was a blow, but *Gott* didn't abandon you. There's a line in Exodus—'The Lord will fight for you. You need only to be still.' To use a modern cliché, you have to roll with the punches. Whatever injustice you feel on your part, it doesn't mean *Gott* isn't there waiting to pick you up and get you back on your feet."

"I guess." She tucked her knees under her chin again and wrapped her arms around them. "I was raised without faith, and it's hard to accept the fact that God cares about each and every one of us."

"Yet He does. That's one of the toughest things for the wider world to accept or understand. Or believe. It's why I came back to the Amish, to my roots. I found it easier to maintain my beliefs by *living* them, not fighting to keep them while living among people who don't share those beliefs."

"I wonder—would it be better for young people not to go on this *rumspringa* in the first place? Maybe it's not such a good thing if they don't come back, like you."

"No. I think it's necessary for young people to get it out of their system. The wider world is like the forbidden fruit, all the more attractive because it's out of reach. By letting them taste it, they can decide for themselves whether they want to accept or reject it. Those who truly want to stay Amish get baptized, which makes for a more unified community."

"But if they don't have the street smarts, they could get hurt by all the evil that's out in the world." She shivered in the warm sun.

"Most of the time, *rumspringas* are pretty mild, comparatively speaking. Most teens don't even leave home, much less go live in the city. Most kids already know whether they want to stay and be baptized, or whether they want to leave. Sure, some kids go wild—I seem to remember a scandal with a drug bust many years ago—but I think the *Englisch* make a bigger deal out of how wild *rumspringa* is than we do."

"Both Sarah and Rachel were like that. They knew they wanted to stay and be baptized. Because of her disability, Rachel didn't want to leave home at all."

"And Ivan and Edith didn't expect her to, if she didn't feel comfortable. Amish parents don't encourage their kids to go crazy and engage in sinful behaviors. They certainly don't condone it. But there has to be some semblance of free choice in the decision to remain Amish. Unforced decisions. Otherwise unhappy adults would sow dissent within the community. In fact—" His eyes twinkled. "Often the goal of a *rumspringa* is to find a spouse."

Leah chuckled. "So that's another myth busted. Everyone always hears about how crazy the kids go. That also explains why you were the oddball, since you left entirely."

"*Ja.* They say a fling with worldliness reminds young people they have a choice about church membership. Knowing they have that choice strengthens their willingness to obey church standards. I didn't want to—that's why I left. I changed my mind, which is why I came back."

She turned serious. "Which is also why you should get it out of your head that I'm an eligible match. Pursuing me as a spouse may well get you banished."

"I've thought of that." He looked over the pond. "And as you say, I only met you a short time ago, hardly the foundation to base a relationship on. At least with Amish youth, they know they share a common denominator of faith and family. But you—you're an unknown. Granted, that's part of the attraction, but in the long run…" His voice trailed off.

"In the long run, I might be a poor choice," she finished for him.

"*Ja*, perhaps."

"Well, at least I know you're not chasing me for my money," she quipped.

His eyes crinkled with humor beneath his curly hair. "Money isn't a big deal with the Amish. No one's wealthy, but no one is desperate either. We all watch out for each other and help anyone in need. Wealth is a distraction from living as *Gott* wants us to live. If you had money, it wouldn't matter how interesting you were. I'd stay away."

She gave a short laugh. "I feel like I'm living in *Alice in Wonderland*. Everything is different."

"I felt the same way when I left the Amish and went to college, then to work. Values I took for granted were suddenly scarce, and values I didn't like were common. I know just how Alice felt." He gave a short chuckle. "I have two favorite Bible verses that guide my work. One is from First Thessalonians and says, 'Make it your ambition to lead a quiet life. You should mind your own business and work with your hands, just as we told you, so that your daily life may win the respect of outsiders and so that you will not be dependent on anybody.'"

Leah gave a little snort of laughter. "That sounds tailor-made for the Amish."

"Ain't so? But it's also why I was willing to accede to the decision of the bishop and the elders when it came to publishing a magazine with a computer. If they felt it would disrupt our lifestyle and not win the respect of outsiders, then I was willing to drop it."

Leah watched the turtle on the log. "You said you had two Bible verses that guide your work. What's the other one?"

"It's from Romans—'We have different gifts, according to the grace given to each of us. If your gift is prophesying, then prophesy in accordance with your faith. If it is serving, then serve. If it is teaching, then teach. If it is to encourage, then give encouragement.

If it is giving, then give generously. If it is to lead, do it diligently. If it is to show mercy, do it cheerfully.'"

Leah cocked her head. "So in other words, whatever talent you have should be used to honor the glory of God."

"Right. No matter how modest or humble."

"I wonder what my talent is, now that I'm no longer a journalist."

"Of course you're still a journalist. You're just no longer a *television* journalist. Now you need to figure out what to do next."

She toyed with the strings on her *kapp.* "Do many outsiders become Amish?"

"No."

"Maybe I should phrase it differently. Do people ever express interest in becoming Amish?"

Isaac gave a small snort of amusement. "Oh, sure. But no one wants to do the work involved."

"Well, it *is* harder physically…"

"No, I don't mean farmwork or carpentry or housework. They don't want to adopt the things important to the Amish. They don't want to give up cell phones or the internet, even if the result is richer friendships. They don't want to give up their secular ways and serve *Gott*, even if the result is peace and saving their soul. They don't want to give up their competitive ways and learn to become cooperative, to bury *self* for the benefits of community. That's a lot of work."

"And to my English ears, it seems overwhelming."

He nodded. "That's why conversions seldom happen. Becoming Amish is not just about dressing up in a costume and keeping your head covered. The clothing has a purpose, a rich meaning, but it's just the outward reflection of the all-encompassing spiritual life we try to lead. It's a lot for most modern women to consider."

"Not a lot of feminists among you, is that it?"

"Nope. This doesn't mean Amish women don't have strong opinions. They do. But just like the men, they must subsume their identities to the community. That's tough for outsiders."

"But I sometimes wonder if it's worth it." She stared over the pond. "But it seems you don't have the same stresses here."

"No. We have stresses, of course, sometimes big ones. The parent who's ill, an accident with an over-turned buggy, the birth of a disabled child, a fire that destroys a house or barn. But overall, I don't believe *Gott* wants us to lead…to lead…" His eyes crinkled with amusement. "To lead lives of quiet desperation."

"You're quoting Thoreau?"

"Yes."

"You're an odd man, Isaac."

"So I've been told by every eligible young woman in the area."

She grew curious. "Are you lonely?"

"Yes and no. No one can really be lonely around here—we're too involved in the community to exclude anyone. But I'm at that point in life where I want to find a wife and have a family. I'm considerably older than most men when they embark on that adventure—and I'm starting to feel left out."

"Hence the reason you're focusing on me."

"That's part of it," he admitted. "But you're right, there are some pretty big obstacles." He rose to his feet and held out his hands to help her up. "Come on, I'm getting hungry. Perhaps you could offer me some dinner."

Leah grasped his hands and stood up. He wasn't much taller than she was, only a few inches. The moment lengthened as he kept her hands in his. His eyes looked dark under the brim of his hat, and for once they didn't sparkle with merriment.

It had been a long time since Leah had been kissed. Romantic entanglements were something she generally avoided. But she wouldn't mind if Isaac took advantage of the situation…

But he didn't.

She wasn't sure if she was relieved or disappointed when he dropped her hands and turned to walk back to the road.

Chapter Ten

On a bright morning a week later, Leah went out to the chicken yard to toss a bowlful of kitchen scraps to the hens. She chuckled as the birds scrambled for the best bits, pecking and squawking at one another.

Suddenly from inside Ivan's workshop, she heard a cry. "Ivan, watch out! Get out of the way!"

A sickening crash, a shriek of alarm from Isaac, screams from the younger boys, and Leah scrambled out of the pen and ran as fast as she could toward the open door of the shop.

Inside, she saw Isaac shove a massive board away from Ivan, who was lying on the floor of the shop. She rushed to his side as Isaac dropped to his knees beside the older man.

Ivan was conscious but looked dazed as she and Isaac helped him sit up.

"What happened?" she asked.

"He was trying to pull that piece of lumber down from up there." Isaac pointed to the low rafters used to store extra boards. "It landed right on his head."

Looking at the huge slab, Leah marveled it hadn't crushed Ivan's skull. She looked at a lump on the top of his head and swallowed hard.

"Ivan, can you talk?" Isaac supported Ivan around his shoulders.

The older man stared straight ahead, dazed. "Uh…"

"Maybe we should get him to his feet." Leah knew nothing about handling medical emergencies.

"No, let's let him sit for a bit." He examined the lump on the top of Ivan's head. It was growing larger, bulging alarmingly. "I told him not to try taking down that board on his own, but he's feeling the pressure of getting this furniture order finished as fast as possible. He's on deadline."

Abruptly Ivan leaned over and got sick. Isaac snatched off his canvas work apron and wiped him down.

"I think we should take him to the hospital." Leah held Ivan's head as he retched again. "I don't like the look of that lump, and head wounds can be dangerous."

Isaac nodded. "If you can watch over him, I'll hitch up the buggy."

Leah looked at the young Byler sons, who stared at their father with horror. "Listen, boys, your dad is going to be okay, but we need to take him to see a doctor. Would you go into the house and let your mother know? But don't go in there screaming and crying. You're both fine young men and I know you won't do that." She smiled in what she hoped was a reassuring fashion.

The children nodded and scampered off.

From a distance she heard sounds of Isaac hitching

up the mare to the buggy. In her arms, Ivan sagged. He was still conscious, but he mumbled incoherently.

In a few moments she heard the sound of pounding footsteps. *"Daed! Daed!"* cried Sarah, dashing into the shop. She dropped to her knees beside her father. Hard on her heels came Rachel, with Edith waddling behind.

Leah directed her words at the older woman. The last thing Edith needed was hysteria, not in her condition. "Just a bump on the head," she said. "I think it's wise to take him to see a doctor, but I think he'll be right as rain in a short time."

"Ivan!" Edith squatted down and nearly lost her balance. Rachel held her steady. "Ivan, can you talk? Are you okay?"

"Hurts," he mumbled, eyes on the floor.

With relief Leah heard the clip-clop of horse hooves as Isaac directed the buggy to the door of the wood shop. "Whoa!" He pulled the animal to a stop and climbed down from the driver's seat. He took command. "Sarah, run into the house and get a pillow. Some towels, too, and a bucket of water half full. Edith, don't worry, we'll have the doctor look him over to make sure he's okay."

Edith straightened up and nodded. Tears streaked down her cheeks, but she held herself erect and spoke calmly. *"Danke*, Isaac. I don't know what I'd do without you here."

"I want you to stay calm. You're carrying a little one who needs you to stay calm. Okay?"

"Ja."

"Leah and I will take him in to Pikeville. We may not be back until late."

Sarah dashed back out, burdened with two pillows and an armful of towels, sloshing water in a bucket.

"*Danke*, Sarah. Leah, let's get him to his feet…"

It took five minutes to maneuver the dazed Ivan into the back of the buggy. Leah climbed in beside him and propped him on pillows. "Hurts, hurts," he mumbled.

"We'll be back as soon as possible," Isaac told Edith. He clucked to the horse and started down the lane.

"How long to get to the hospital?" Leah put her arm around Ivan's shoulders. "Don't fall asleep, Ivan!"

"About half an hour to get there. This is when I'd love a phone and a car."

"Amen to that."

Concentrating on Ivan, she hardly noticed the transition from rural to small town. Isaac directed the horse with grim concentration as he avoided anything that might unduly jostle his passenger. When they finally made it to the hospital parking lot, he pulled the horse to a stop, hopped out and tied the animal to a hitching post under the shade of several trees, put there for the area's Amish population. "Stay here. I'm going to get someone with a gurney or a wheelchair," he told her.

Left alone, Leah gave Ivan a tiny shake. "We're here, Ivan. We'll get your head looked at right away. Don't fall asleep, okay?" She continued to chatter foolishness until the hospital staff arrived with a wheelchair.

They whisked Ivan away for examination. Leah collapsed on a chair in the waiting room while Isaac spoke to the reception desk. Then he came and sat next to her. He dropped his head into his hands. "That's a sound I never want to hear again, that board hitting Ivan's head."

"You said he was in a hurry?"

"*Ja.* This furniture order has been giving him some troubles, and they wanted it sooner than he anticipated. It's one of the reasons I've been working for him lately. His boys are too young to operate the power tools, and he needed help." He straightened up and leaned against the seat back.

"What now? I can't imagine he'll be in any shape to get back to work right away."

"No. I'll have to take it over." Lines of tension tightened around his mouth.

"I hope Edith doesn't fret too much."

"Edith is a good one to put her trust in the Lord during an emergency."

Trust in the Lord. Leah found herself praying—praying that Ivan's head wound was not serious and that he would suffer no long-term problems.

Within half an hour, a doctor emerged into the waiting room. "Are you with Ivan Byler?" he asked.

Isaac jerked to his feet. "Yes. I work with him in his wood shop. I'm Isaac Sommer, and this is Leah Porte, a guest of the Bylers."

The doctor shook hands. "He'll be fine. Took a nasty blow, as you know, but I've seen worse. I wanted to go over recovery procedures with you."

"I assume he's off work for a while?"

"Absolutely. He's going to have some balance issues for some time, and probably some spatial ones as well— depth perception and the like. It's critical to keep him away from any power tools or he could get hurt. He's going to suffer headaches for about a week or more, and he'll get tired easily. Oddly enough, I don't recommend letting him take naps during the day. Just let him sleep at night as always. This will more or less force him to stay on a regular sleep schedule."

"Will he be on any pain medication?"

"Just over-the-counter, non-aspirin pain medicine." The doctor tapped the side of his head. "He's not likely to have much memory of the event itself, so don't let that alarm you."

"It was a scary situation." Isaac passed a hand over his face, and Leah realized how fond of his boss Isaac was, and how much the accident had frightened him. "A huge board just fell off some rafters and landed on his head. I'm surprised it didn't knock him cold, or even kill him."

"The human skull is pretty tough." The doctor smiled. "And the human body is resilient. Keep him quiet for a few weeks and he should be fine."

"His wife is expecting a baby, so this should be a relief to her."

"I imagine so." The doctor fished into a coat pocket and extracted a business card. "I know you're not likely to have a phone, but here's my contact information if you need to reach me."

"Thank you, Doctor." Isaac took the card.

"He'll be ready to go in a few minutes. We'll bring him out in a wheelchair."

Isaac collapsed back into a chair, and Leah sat down next to him. "You okay?" she asked. He looked so shaken.

"I think it's just catching up to me how near a thing it was." Isaac closed his eyes and pinched the bridge of his nose. Leah's throat closed as she realized he was fighting tears. "It was bad when I lost my own father, but at least I was an adult. When I think of how worse off Edith and the children would be if something were to happen to Ivan…"

She put her arm around his shoulders, and he leaned into her and let out one sob before he controlled himself. Her heart melted at his vulnerability.

"He'll be all right," she soothed. "I'm just thankful you were there when it happened, so you could help him right away. You're a good man in an emergency, Isaac."

He nodded and fished a handkerchief out of his pocket, then straightened up and mopped his face. "Sorry," he mumbled. "I usually don't lose it like that."

"There's no need to apologize, Isaac," she reassured him and gave his shoulders a little squeeze. "It's been a rough morning. You did well."

A door opened across the waiting room, and a nurse backed through, pulling a wheelchair with Ivan sitting upright. The nurse turned the chair around, and Ivan offered them a wan smile. "Still here," he offered.

Relief flooded Leah. He was pale, but if he was well enough to crack weak jokes, that was half the battle.

From Isaac's expression, Leah would never guess he had broken down a minute before. He rose, smiled and squatted next to the older man, looking only concerned and attentive. "You gave us a good scare. Don't do that again, hear?"

"*Ja*, sure."

Isaac rose and looked at the nurse. "Can we take him home?"

"Yes. Keep him quiet, of course, and you may have to assist him walking to your car."

"Buggy," Isaac corrected with a ghost of a smile.

"Buggy, then." The nurse appeared unfazed.

Isaac looked at Leah. "I'll go get the horse." He strode out of the waiting room into the parking lot.

She nodded and sat down in a chair next to Ivan. "Edith was a bit worried about you," she chattered to cover her concern. "She'll be so glad you're still in one piece."

"I have a headache," he admitted. "A bad one. And I'm tired. But the doctor said I shouldn't take any naps."

"That's what he told us too. Follow the doctor's orders!"

"Do you have pain relievers at home?" asked the nurse.

"I don't know," she confessed. "I'm staying as a guest at the Bylers' house, and I've never rummaged through their medicine cabinet."

"Let me get you a small sample bottle. It's free," said the nurse. "That will tide you over until you know for sure."

By the time the nurse found the sample bottle, Isaac had pulled the horse and buggy around to the emergency room's awning. Together with the nurse, she helped Ivan into the buggy and sat down next to him.

"Avoid bumps as best you can," the nurse advised Isaac. "Goodbye, Mr. Byler. Take care of yourself."

"Thank you, miss."

Isaac directed the horse toward home, going as gently as he could. Ivan spoke and seemed lucid. "I don't remember what happened, but I'm grateful you two were there to help me."

"Ivan, don't worry about the furniture order." Isaac spoke over his shoulder, his eyes on the road. "I'll take over and finish it. The only thing I'm going to let you do is inspect my work each night to make sure it's progressing the way you want it."

"*Ja, danke*, Isaac." Ivan dropped his head in his hands a moment before straightening up.

"We'll get you some medicine when you get home." It wasn't hard for Leah to read his symptoms. He was in pain. "And I'm sure Edith will want to fuss over you."

Once Isaac pulled the buggy in front of the Byler home, Edith and the children poured out, ready to fuss just as Leah predicted.

"Each of you take an arm and escort him slowly," Isaac instructed Edith and Sarah. "Obviously he's to take it easy for a while, but the doctor said he might be dizzy, and I don't want him falling."

"Actually, Edith, let me take his other arm." Leah climbed down from the buggy. "You've already been under enough strain."

The older woman nodded. *"Danke."*

Walking like an old man, Ivan shuffled toward the porch and leaned heavily on Leah and Sarah as he climbed the steps. Edith waddled behind, one hand resting on her girth.

In the house, Leah helped Ivan to a kitchen chair, where he collapsed and smiled wanly. "Don't worry, I'm not on death's door," he assured his wife.

She, too, dropped into a chair, her eyes trembling with tears, but she spoke briskly. "You gave us quite a scare."

Ivan covered his wife's hands. "Thanks be to *Gott* that Isaac was able to bring me to the hospital." He looked at Leah. "You too."

Isaac came clattering into the house. "Ivan, I'll be in the shop. Don't worry about that order—I'll do whatever I can to make the deadline." His face held an expression of grim determination.

"*Ja, danke*, Isaac." Ivan closed his eyes a moment. "I don't know what I'd do without you."

Over the next week, Leah watched Isaac work himself into the ground. He arrived early at the Bylers' farm. He left late. He barely took time to finish the midday meal Edith insisted he eat with them. The shadows under his eyes darkened day by day.

She watched Isaac grow more and more serious, with a grim expression more often than not. It wasn't just his concern over Ivan. The older man was recuperating fine and was able to supervise Isaac's progress from afar.

It wasn't like Isaac to be so worried. The sparkle and enthusiasm had left his eyes, and worry had taken over. Why? It wasn't just filling the furniture order. She knew by now he was a fine woodworker. No, it was something else.

She confronted him in the shop one afternoon. "What's wrong?"

"What do you mean?" He ran a planer over a board.

"You seem like you're burning the candle at both ends. You're more stressed than I've ever seen you. Why?"

He straightened and ran a hand over his face in a gesture of weariness. "I'm on two deadlines," he admitted. "This order for Ivan must be done by Friday after next, and ironically I'm trying to get the fall issue of the magazine to the printers by the same date so it can be printed and mailed."

"Let me guess. You've been working through the night on the magazine and during the day on the tools." That explained the dark circles under his eyes. "Why didn't you tell me? I can help—not with the woodworking, of course, but on the magazine."

"Because you made it clear you weren't interested."

She flinched. So that's what he thought of her.

In that moment, Leah knew it was time to step up and push her ego out of the way. "I can take over the magazine," she offered. "If you bring your laptop, I can work here in the Bylers' kitchen. That way you can check what I'm doing mid-day, and you'll be nearby if I have a question."

His jaw dropped. "You would do that?"

"You need help because you're helping the Bylers during a time of crisis. The Bylers took me in during my own time of crisis. So, it's payback time."

Enthusiasm lit up his eyes. Leah didn't realize how much she'd missed it until it returned. *"Danke,"* he said simply. He glanced at a clock nailed over the shop door. "I'm going to borrow a horse and ride home and get the laptop right now. Tell Ivan I'll be back shortly." He placed the planer on the board and trotted out the shop door.

Leah shook her head and smiled. It seemed she had a new job.

Chapter Eleven

Leah threw herself into her new routine.

She got up early. She assisted the women with their work. She helped with laundry and hanging clothes on the line. She learned to strain milk. She aided in making butter. She picked up the finer points of kneading bread. She weeded the garden. She picked strawberries and made preserves. She swept the house and the porches. And she worked—for many hours each day—on the magazine.

In the evening she gathered with the family to listen while Ivan read a chapter or two from the German Bible. While she was able to catch some of the majestic cadence, she learned to follow in the English Bible she'd been lent, as long as she had enough time to find the chapters before he started.

And afterward, she wrote.

"I'm short several articles this issue," Isaac admitted on that first day she worked on the magazine. "A few people said they would send things, but they either changed their minds or they never got around to it." He quirked an eyebrow. "So if you're interested, I would still value your input as a newcomer among the Amish. Your views on how things are tackled would be invaluable."

So in the evenings, while the adults read or knitted or chatted, while the children played games or read books, she parked herself with a lamp at her elbow and wrote the articles that were forming in her mind as she went through the day's work.

She also started a diary, figuring the impressions she formed might prove useful one day.

"What are you writing?" Edith asked one evening, her knitting needles clicking.

"This time an article on making cheese," replied Leah, pausing with her pen in the air. "The first time I saw Rachel making it, I was dumbfounded. I didn't even know you could *make* cheese at home."

"How else is it done?" asked Edith.

"By huge factories who then sell it in stores," replied Leah. "It all tastes the same."

"Sad."

This was another factor Leah discovered as her involvement and understanding of the Amish deepened. The wider world held very little appeal to those who had been baptized and remained in the community. Even Sarah, as lovely as she was, had no interest in further enhancing her appearance with cosmetics or fashions, a subject driven home one day by a conversation Leah had with her. A young woman with an aversion to shopping was so unusual that Leah found it hard to believe.

"Shopping for what?" asked Sarah, when Leah broached the subject. "For clothes? What I'm wearing is always in fashion. Electronics? From what I've heard, they do more harm than good."

The Amish didn't feel deprived at what they were missing, Leah concluded. They were satisfied with what they had. It was such a different attitude from the normal consumer-driven *Englisch* culture she had left behind that it took some getting used to.

"Don't you ever get tired?" she gasped to Edith on the following Saturday night. Her hair felt stringy and dirty, and she'd spent a hot afternoon working over the cookstove.

"Of course." Edith waddled with her increasing girth to the sink and began washing some early carrots. "But work is an honor. Labor is a gift. It's not something to avoid, but something to embrace. That way, rest is sweeter."

That was another attitude Leah had a hard time embracing. Work never ceased.

Yet within that work was skill. In fact, work involved far more skill than appeared on the surface. Leah first approached her stay with the Amish with a mental image of drudgery, of backs eternally bent over their crops, spurning anything modern that might lighten their burdens.

It took some time to realize that while modern technology was absent, it didn't mean drudgery ruled the day. In fact, she learned life without modern conveniences consisted not of brawn alone but of human wit and ingenuity. She watched the skillful ways Sarah and Rachel applied a hoe to the weeds in the garden, or flipped a sheet for hanging or waited until the dew dried on the lawn before attempting to mow with a push mower. There was unconscious skill in these decisions—and that skill made the job easier.

"It's also the sense of sharing," said Rachel during another conversation Leah initiated on the subject. "Have you noticed that very few people work alone? Tasks are almost always shared. Many hands make light work, and that includes conversation to help pass the time."

Leah was helping Rachel sweep the walkway when she brought up the topic. She was so startled at the obviousness of the concept that she stalled in her task.

"You're right!" she exclaimed. "I don't think I realized it before!"

Rachel chuckled. "You're funny. I think the *Englisch* believe there's some magic involved in how industrious we tend to be, but it's simply because we like working together that we can get so much done. Even *Daed* has the boys to talk to while he works in his shop, or Isaac when he's here. It makes everyone's work easier and faster when the burden can be shared, don't you think? Isn't it more fun to sweep this walkway together than it might be alone?"

"Absolutely." Leah was silent for a few strokes of the broom. "It's so different," she said at last. "Different from *Englisch* society. I grew up thinking independence is the ultimate goal. I shouldn't need help from anyone, and if I did, I would pay them to help me. But here, it's like the opposite of independence. It's *dependence*. And there again, it shows how different the outside world is. Dependence is considered unhealthy and unnatural."

"Maybe it's a factor of who you're dependent *on*,"

said Rachel. "There's no shame in asking for help from family or church."

"The trouble is so many *Englisch* people have no family or church."

"Like you."

"Yes, like me. That's why this whole community thing is so hard to get used to."

"Do you find it oppressive?"

Leah worked her broom. "Maybe a little. If you're used to being alone a lot, then never being alone takes some getting used to. But overall I like it. It seems…it seems *joyous* somehow."

Rachel grinned. "Good word," she replied. "That's often how I feel. Joyous."

Joyous. Now that she'd said the word aloud, it seemed very apt for so many situations. The Bylers—and everyone else she met—took joy in their work.

"So many people object to labor, somehow thinking it interferes with better things." Edith kneaded some bread dough as Leah broached the subject one afternoon. "But this *is* our job, our career. It's what we do. We don't try to hurry through it and get it out of the way so we can get other stuff done. This *is* the stuff we need to get done." She swiped her cheek and left a small dusting of flour. "Me, I like what I do. This is my career, I guess you could call it."

"And you do it well," replied Leah.

That night Leah lay in bed, her hands under her head, and stared at the dark ceiling. She thought about Isaac.

Since Ivan's accident, she had seen another side to the man. He was cool under pressure. He didn't complain about a double workload. He kept his humor and his common sense. Working more closely with him on the magazine, she better understood his vision and his plans.

Altogether he was a very attractive package, both inside and out.

It was difficult to admit she was reacting to Isaac the way she responded to any girlish crush. But she was not a girl, and Isaac was not a boy. They were grown adults and came from wildly different backgrounds. All the gentle warnings she'd received so far weren't so much because anyone thought she would be a poor match for him; they were simply grounded on the basis that she didn't share his faith.

Listening to the sounds of frogs and crickets coming through her open bedroom window, she wondered what it would be like to stay here. Always. In some ways she felt as if she was living in a time warp—it was hard not to, reading by oil lamp and canning raspberry jam— but by now she knew the Amish way of life was more than skin-deep. It was built on a foundation of the most profound faith.

Since she'd arrived, the growing possibility that God existed and actually cared about her had started to grow, like a young plant being tenderly nourished by the nightly Bible readings, the quiet faith of those around her and her own biblical explorations. Having never really paid attention to the Bible, it was a revelation to her.

But she believed her future wasn't here, on this quiet and peaceful farm amid these industrious and welcoming people. Once it was deemed safe, she would return to the English world. She would remove her *kapp* and apron and don a business suit and…do what?

That was the question that remained unanswered. She supposed she'd stay in journalism somehow, but with a death threat hanging over her, she could have neither her face nor her name associated with anything.

She had no idea how to fill the big gaping void in front of her.

Chapter Twelve

On a hot and humid afternoon, Leah set off toward Isaac's house. Summer had matured into an explosion of wild tiger lilies on the roadside, along with black-eyed Susans and daisies.

The climate itself was so lush and verdant compared to dry Southern California that Leah didn't even mind the humidity. Everything was so green!

"*Guder nammidaag*, Eleanor," she greeted Isaac's mother at the door. "How are you feeling today?"

"*Guder nammidaag*. About the same." Eleanor never complained about the hip pain Leah knew plagued her. "Have you come to work on Isaac's computer?"

"Yes." Leah stepped into the coolness of the living room. "We're finalizing the issue. Hello, Isaac," she added as she spied him seated at the kitchen table.

He rose. "*Guder nammidaag*. How are your typing fingers today?"

She gave an exaggerated stretch of her arms and hands before her. "Rarin' to go!"

"You should see what I got in the mail today. It's

too late to put it in this issue, but I thought you'd get a chuckle out of it." He grinned and handed her a piece of paper. "This is from a seven-year-old boy. We'll have to correct for spelling."

The short poem was penned in purple crayon and was creative in its use of spelling. Yet it had a sweet charm. She chuckled. "Not sure we should correct the spelling errors. Half the cuteness here is in how he wrote it. What about printing a corrected version of the poem, but then including a photo of the original right beneath it?"

"*Ja*, good idea. But as I said, this will have to wait until the next issue." He laid the paper aside. "Your articles look good, and I'm grateful you wrote them. No regrets?"

"None." Sitting at the laptop, Leah pulled up the two articles she had contributed to the issue. "Doing laundry by hand, and making mozzarella cheese. I think they're both informative. I figure if I'm going to cover something as a journalist, no matter what the subject is, I'll do the most professional job I can."

"It's obvious why you were at the top of your field."

She glanced at him, but he was leafing through a manila folder containing papers. His words didn't bring the accustomed stab of pain.

Instead she pointed to the computer. "After all this work, what have you done to increase circulation?"

"We try to make sure every store in every Plain community has copies to sell." He closed the folder and laid it on the table. "Mostly things have spread through word of mouth."

"Have you reconsidered setting up a website?"

"Not really. I wouldn't know how anyway."

She shook her head. "It's a beautiful magazine, and if you want to increase the number of copies you sell, you really should have something online for people to read. It doesn't have to be anything fancy, just an information-only spot, but it could help you sell a lot more copies."

"Up to this point, the magazine has been a one-man business." He looked troubled. "You're suggesting making it bigger."

"Don't you want to?"

"Yes. No. I don't know." He scrubbed a hand over his face. "As you found out the hard way, it's a tremendous amount of work as it is, especially when it gets close to publishing each issue, but it pulls in enough income to make it worthwhile."

"But increasing the circulation wouldn't appreciably change the work you already do, which is gathering articles and doing the layout. It just means more people will see it."

"And then it snowballs. From a website comes digital-only access. Then comes social media. Then comes advertisements, often from sources not suitable to Plain People." He gave a small shudder. "I've seen some of those online network ads. They're horrible. Then comes expanding the email subscriber list and sending out email newsletters and the like. Then there are all the other associated internet possibilities— YouTube videos and podcasts and such." He shook his head. "No."

"So you *do* understand how to grow a magazine." It seemed strange to hear this Amish man spouting the intricacies of modern marketing strategies. "You just choose not to do it."

"Right. You have to understand—I'm walking a fine line. It's bad enough I work on a computer to get the magazine out, which is shocking enough for this community. I have to keep things low-key and acceptable to Amish standards if I'm going to be allowed to continue running the magazine. Or else I might experience a *bann*, which could lead to *meidung*. Shunning."

"I see your point," she mused. "I just find it interesting to meet someone whose goal isn't massive growth and wild success."

"The magazine *is* growing. But it's growing because it contains information people want and like. Beautiful photographs, the simple life, rural living. It appeals to people already living this lifestyle, or who want to. That's why your article on doing laundry by hand is so perfect. It's not so much for the Amish, because they already know how. But you came from an urban background and doubtless had never seen it done before."

"Of course not."

"And you'd be surprised how many people—I think they're called back-to-the-landers—want to know how to live a rural life without breaking out the old-fashioned washboard to get their clothes clean." He smiled. "Maybe by your journalistic standards, laundry is considered a trivial and ridiculous subject, but I assure you it's not."

"Having experienced the contrast between a modern washing machine and a hand-powered one, I agree." She smiled. "You know, it's funny. I find my mind awhirl with so many article ideas, far more than you could ever use for your magazine. I just find myself amazed at this life, one I never really knew existed. And I think you're right—there are a lot of people who would want to know everything from how to preserve meat to how to raise respectful kids. I guess that's why I was pushing the idea of expanding the magazine. It seems like the logical way to get this information out there."

"A book."

"Excuse me?"

"It occurs to me you should write a book. Lots of people have written of the culture shock of going from Amish to *Englisch*, but I don't think anyone's done the opposite—written what it's like to go from *Englisch* to Amish. You're seeing things through the eyes of an outsider while living among us. It's a unique perspective."

"But I'm not Amish."

"No, but you're living the lifestyle for the time being."

"Are the Amish allowed to write books?"

"Of course! Lots of them do."

"Hmm." It was a valuable tip, and she mentally filed it away for later. "But I still think you need a website. You can make it information only—just something simple on what the magazine is about, where to buy copies and how to submit material. I can do it for you, if you like. No phone number, of course, and a warning next to the email that it may take some time to respond."

He looked wary. "Is it hard to do?"

"Only hard to the extent it will have to be done from the library in Pikeville, where there's internet service. But there are many free website design sites online. If I had the copy—the text—written out in advance, I could probably register a domain name and pull together a basic information-only website in a few hours."

"I'll think about it. I'm still not convinced it's necessary, but you make a persuasive argument."

"It wouldn't change anything, except to make it easier for new readers to find you and new writers to send you stuff."

Eleanor limped into the kitchen. "Isaac, *lieb*, could you fetch me some canned pork from the cellar for supper?"

"Ja, ofkoors." He departed, and Leah was left alone with his mother for a few minutes.

"I'm so glad you're helping him with the magazine." Eleanor smiled. "He struggles with the computer, even though the magazine looks so good in the end."

"It's no trouble," said Leah. "As you can imagine, I grew up using them, so to me they're easy. I used to be a journalist, so I'm even familiar with the particular software he uses."

"That's *gut*." As Isaac's footsteps clattered back up the stairs, Eleanor gave what sounded like a blessing. "I hope this works out for the long term. Thank you," she added as Isaac handed her a quart jar of meat.

Leah continued work with Isaac, finalizing the issue's details as the evening sun lowered in the sky. Eleanor bustled about the kitchen, cooking.

"You must stay for supper." The older woman stirred a pot.

"Thank you—I am hungry," she admitted.

"Let me milk the cows and I'll be ready," Isaac told his mother. He grabbed two stainless steel buckets and left the kitchen.

"How many cows do you have?" Leah asked Eleanor as she turned off the laptop and cleared the table.

"Two. It's all we need with just the two of us living here."

"Edith said it's traditional for the parents' farm to go to the youngest son. And that's Isaac?"

"*Ja*. But he's not a farmer. My second-youngest son, he farms the land. All we keep is some pigs and chickens and cows, and of course a garden and an orchard. Right now, because of my hip, I'm limited to the house, so a lot of the work falls on Isaac. Then he has the magazine, of course, and he's a leatherworker like his father. He makes bridles and harnesses."

"A leatherworker! I didn't know that! I thought he worked with wood." Again, the journalist in her sat upright.

"He does, but leatherwork is his specialty."

Leah wanted to touch on Eleanor's need for a hip replacement, but she knew it wasn't her place to inquire. Despite Eleanor's fragile appearance, Leah sensed a deep core of steel in the older woman. If she didn't want surgery, she didn't want surgery.

"Where are the dishes?" she asked instead. "I'll set the table."

Eleanor directed her to the appropriate locations, and Leah set the table while the older woman finished preparing the meal.

When Isaac finally came in with two buckets full of milk, Eleanor strained it while Isaac washed and sterilized the buckets. Now that she was used to the Bylers' industriousness and large number of hands to help with the work, she realized just how busy these two—especially Isaac, since Eleanor was unable to do any out-side work—must be.

She finally sat at the table after Isaac carried the food over. She bowed her head, mentally said a prayer and waited for the others to finish their blessings before making a proposal.

"You know," she said, "I'm sort of a fifth wheel at the Bylers'. Ivan's back on his feet and in the shop, and Sarah and Rachel don't really need my help. What do you say I come here every day and do some of the outside work? I'm pretty handy now at things like laundry and weeding the garden. I'd be happy to lend a hand."

She saw the look of surprise between mother and son. "Thank you, Leah," said Eleanor at last. "I would be grateful."

"I'll confirm everything with Edith first, but I'm sure she won't mind. Besides…" She grinned. "It would be a chance to hone my skills on my own. I need a lot of honing."

"I would appreciate it." Isaac's voice held a note of surprise and pleasure.

"Let's assume I can start tomorrow," continued Leah. "What would be best for me to work on first?"

Gardening seemed the highest priority. "The raspberries are full ripe, and it's hard for Isaac to keep up with them," said Eleanor. "If you pick and then bring them in, I can preserve them."

"Isaac, why don't you show me around the garden after we finish eating?" suggested Leah. "That way I'll know where all the fruits and vegetables are. And, Eleanor, where would I find such things as buckets and baskets?"

Her offer seemed to breach any walls that existed with Eleanor. If there was one thing Leah had learned since coming to stay with the Bylers, it was that labor was the currency of the community. Exchanging labor was not only a means of getting more work done, but it was also a social lubricant that offered endless opportunities for visiting and friendship.

After the meal, Eleanor shooed Leah outside with Isaac, who led the way to a broad, verdant garden.

"It's gotten a bit away from me since *Mamm*'s hip has slowed her down," he admitted as he toured her around.

Leah was now familiar enough with the plants growing in the Bylers' garden to identify beans, carrots, peas, strawberries, and all the other types of fruits and vegetables. But in contrast to the diligent efforts of the Bylers, this garden was weedier and more neglected. Still fruitful, just less tidy.

"Here are the raspberries," said Isaac, stopping before a raised bed with leafy branches arching over, laden with berries. "I've only managed to pick about a quart a day—as you can see, not from a lack of fruit, but because I have so much else to do."

Leah slipped a berry off its stem and popped it into her mouth. "Looks like these are thornless berries, just like the Bylers'."

"Yes. Much easier for picking."

Leah looked around the garden. In some ways she was excited by the prospect of having this as her little domain, bringing to it some of the order and loveliness of the Bylers' garden. She was learning something surprising about herself: she enjoyed manual labor. It gave her a sense of accomplishment she hadn't often found in journalism work. "I'll start tomorrow," she repeated.

"Thank you," said Isaac. "This will be a big help."

On the walk back to the Bylers', Leah reflected on the tasks done by both men and women in the Amish community. Eleanor's inability to get anything done outdoors, since her walk was unsteady and painful, meant tasks normally designated for women had to be done by Isaac, in addition to his own work. "Many hands make light work," Rachel had said, and it was clear what happened when those hands weren't available.

"Oh, of course!" exclaimed Edith after Leah returned home and explained her plan to the older woman. "How awful of me—I didn't think about how much help she might need! I'll send Sarah and Rachel too."

"No, don't. I know this sounds odd, but I want to see if I can work the garden all by myself. The plants are all thriving…they just need a lot of weeding and cultivating, and some things need harvesting right away, like those raspberries. Give me a week or so and let me see what I can do."

"How different you are from just a month ago when you first came." Edith chuckled. "You're no longer the bewildered beginner. Now you're a woman on a mission. It's nice to see."

And so Leah began a daily "commute," as she jokingly termed it, walking to the Sommers' home every morning. That first day, she picked four quarts of raspberries and deposited them in the kitchen for Eleanor, then seized a hoe and began removing the biggest and most disfiguring weeds from between rows of carrots.

It took a couple of hours before the hoe work was done, then she crouched down and started pulling weeds from between the carrot plants themselves. Eleanor called her in for dinner, then she went straight back outside. By the time she was ready to leave for the evening, the carrot patch was flawless.

She didn't brag about the neatness of the rows. That was not the Amish way. Her work would be noticed. And while neither Isaac nor Eleanor would say anything about it, their estimation of her would rise.

The hours of solitary weeding gave her time to think, especially about her future. She thought about what it would be like to stay here in Pikeville, among the Amish. Could she? She now understood manual labor was welcomed and not avoided, and it surprised her how gratifying she found it. But was this something she could do forever? Could she forsake any future in journalism and remain here indefinitely?

The biggest obstacle about becoming Amish was turning out not to be the work or lack of modern amenities, but the faith required. In a gradual process, she was coming to realize God was not a remote and mythical figure; He was here and present in the everyday.

As she got home one evening, laden with blueberries Eleanor insisted on giving her, Rachel commented, "I'm ashamed how little thought I've given Eleanor. I really wish she would just have her surgery."

"Does she not want it?" Leah popped a berry into her mouth.

"I think deep down she just hopes she'll get better on her own. But she's not. She's getting worse. From what

I've heard, hip replacements are common and make a huge difference for a person."

"That's what I've heard too. It doesn't sound like money is the issue, since your mother told me everyone will pitch in to pay the bills. It sounds like it's just a matter of convincing her."

"*Ja*, and it's not our place to do that. Either Isaac, or one of her other children, are in the best position to talk to her about it."

Leah wondered how long Eleanor could cope without the surgery. It also made her admire Isaac all the more for the way he took care of his mother.

Chapter Thirteen

Early September dawned. The days were growing cooler and the summer humidity was starting to lessen when Edith went into labor.

"There's time yet," she explained to a panicked Leah, when she discovered the older woman leaning into the kitchen counter and panting. "But I wouldn't mind if you fetched Ivan for me. He can get the midwife."

Leah fled out the door and into the workshop. "Ivan, Ivan!" she gasped.

Ivan paused in the act of running a planer over a piece of wood. He stared at her. "What's wrong?"

"It's Edith! She's in labor."

"Oh. Okay." Calmly he laid his tool aside and un-hooked his canvas work apron. It was all Leah could do to keep from shrieking "Hurry up!"

Anxiously she trotted into the kitchen, Ivan walking behind her, to find Edith sitting on a chair with her hands over her belly and her eyes closed.

"Is it time?" Ivan bent over his wife.

Her eyes still closed, she nodded. "Would you mind fetching Elizabeth?" she asked.

Leah knew that was the name of the midwife.

"Of course. I'll get Sarah and Rachel in here, as well." He quirked an eye at Leah and winked. "Someone has to stay calm."

He strolled outside, and Leah heard him calling his older daughters from the garden. In fact, all six children came clamoring inside, but Rachel took charge. "Eliza, take the boys over to the Millers' and stay there until we come get you," she said. "*Mamm*, are you ready to lie down or do you want to walk for a while?"

"Walk, I think. *Danke*."

Both older girls were calm, far calmer than she was—but then, Leah realized, they had doubtless been with their mother numerous times when she gave birth.

"I'll be back shortly!" called Ivan from outside. He clucked to the horse he'd hooked up to the buggy and trotted down the road.

"Would—would you like some tea or something?" Leah felt helpless as another contraction came over Edith and she leaned over the table, her face contorted.

"N-no, thank you," panted Edith. "Relax, child. I'm the one in labor, not you."

Leah dropped the dish towel she'd been pleating into a mass. "I've never been around a woman about to give birth before."

"Really? Well, this isn't my first go-round. I usually don't take too long either. What you could do, please, is start some water heating. Elizabeth always likes fresh hot water. Rachel, dear, when you have a moment, would you fetch the baby clothes?"

Glad to do something to help, Leah stoked the stove and heaved a pot on top, then filled it with water and put a lid on.

Rachel got her mother to her feet. "Up you go," she said. "Let's walk."

Arm in arm, the short young woman and the taller older woman trod around the kitchen. Well, Edith waddled and looked cheerful, despite the strain on her face. "I wonder if it will be a boy or a girl," she mused.

"Do you have a preference?" asked Leah.

"Of course not. So far the Lord has given me equal numbers of both, so I couldn't be happier. Whatever He sends this time will be a blessing."

"How far away does the midwife live?"

"Only about two miles. Ivan will be back soon."

But the minutes that ticked by didn't seem short to Leah. Edith paused every so often and bent over, panting, as another contraction hit. But she refused to get into bed, insisting she was better off moving around. Knowing nothing about the issue, Leah didn't push—especially since neither Sarah nor Rachel thought this was anything unusual.

"Will you be with your mother when she gives birth?" she asked Rachel.

The younger woman shook her head. "There are some things daughters shouldn't see their own mothers do. I've been with some women in labor, but not *Mamm*." She smiled. "But when Sarah has her first baby, I hope I'm there!"

"Sarah, get the birth bag," instructed Edith.

Sarah disappeared into the basement and emerged with a nylon duffel bag, which she put on the table.

At last, Leah heard the welcome clip-clop of a returning horse and buggy, and within minutes a hearty, plump woman bustled into the kitchen and took charge. Clucking in *Deitsch*, she sat Edith in a chair and felt her belly. She brought the birth bag into the bedroom, along with a hefty bag of her own supplies Ivan carried behind her. Then she whisked the expecting mother into the bedroom and closed the door.

"And now we wait." Ivan poured himself a cup of coffee and sat down at the table.

"Will you go in when she's about to give birth?" inquired Leah. She also sat, too boneless to stand.

"*Ja*, of course. But for now, the midwife needs to make some examinations, and that's best done in private."

"Seven children," mused Leah. "That seems like such a large number."

Ivan looked surprised. "It's what *Gott* gives us. Each and every one of them is a blessing of riches."

In the three months since she'd arrived, she knew Ivan spoke the truth. Children were cherished among the Amish. They weren't viewed as inconveniences interfering with a career. They were seen as the natural result of the love between husband and wife.

She heard Edith groan from inside the bedroom, but no dramatic screams or cries rent the air. After a few minutes, the bedroom door opened and the midwife poked her head out. "Ivan, she's near time if you'd like to come in."

Ivan shuffled to his feet and went in to support his wife during her travail.

Leah continued to sit at the kitchen table, watching in some bemusement as Sarah and Rachel went about their tasks. Sarah wore something of a glow on her face. "Someday, that will be me. I can't wait for my first baby."

"And since I won't be having any, I can't wait to hold him," grinned Rachel.

Leah realized she was tense, her muscles clenched as if she were the one in labor. She made a deliberate effort to relax. The minutes ticked by.

Suddenly she heard a subdued flurry of activity...and then a baby's thin wailing cry came through the door.

The sisters exchanged grins.

Rachel dropped clean towels into a large bowl and poured steaming water from the stove over them. When Elizabeth opened the door again, she was ready and handed the woman the bowl.

"Danke." Elizabeth smiled. "You have a beautiful baby sister." She closed the door.

"Ah, that's wonderful," sighed Rachel. She made herself a cup of tea and sat opposite Leah at the table.

"Everyone's so calm," commented Leah. "In the city, having a baby is a huge thing. It starts with baby showers and birth announcements and ends with hospital rooms and doctors." She grew curious. "Do Amish women ever give birth in hospitals? What happens if there's an emergency?"

"Some women use hospitals, but it's expensive, and why go if there's nothing wrong?" countered Sarah. "But yes, emergencies happen. A couple years ago, Penny Miller needed to be transferred to a hospital, but the baby died." She looked grave. "It was very sad.

But she's pregnant again, so this time they'll go to the hospital first."

Elizabeth came out again. "Is there some hot water?" she inquired.

"Ja." Rachel stood up. "I'll bring it."

"Pretty little girl," commented the midwife. She took a small bag from her apron pocket. "Please use this to make some tea. It helps healing."

Sarah took the herbs and prepared tea. Leah dipped hot water into buckets and placed them outside the bedroom door.

Within half an hour, Elizabeth opened the door. "Come in and meet your sister."

Edith looked wan but happy, lying tucked in bed. Next to her, Ivan sat in a rocking chair with the tiny infant in his arms.

"What will you name her?" Sarah bent to take the baby in her arms. "Oh, she's *wunnerschee.*"

"Your mother and I thought Charity Anne," said Ivan.

"That's lovely. Hello, Charity." Rachel touched the baby's face with a gentle finger.

Ivan got out of the rocking chair, and Sarah sat down, cuddling the infant. A peaceful expression passed over her face. Rachel squatted at her feet, peering at her new baby sister.

"How do you feel, Edith?" asked Leah.

"Tired but elated," she replied. "Glad it's over and the baby is healthy."

"Leah, would you like to hold her?" asked Sarah.

"May I?"

"Of course. Sit down." Sarah rose and swapped

places with Leah, who sank into the rocker and took the infant. "Here, like this. Make sure you support her head in the crook of your arm. That's right."

Instinctively Leah began to rock. As she looked at the tiny red face, a thrill came over her—warm waves of love for this tiny child birthed so miraculously in this humble bedroom. Her eyes grew moist. Could she ever do this, have a baby half this wonderful?

"My turn?" Rachel finally asked. Leah looked up to see the young woman standing nearby, clearly anxious to hold her baby sister.

"I'm sorry." She rose and traded places. "I've never held a newborn before. She's amazing!"

Rachel chuckled as she sank into the chair and took her sister with experienced arms. "It never gets old," she admitted.

She looked at Rachel's face, different because of her genetic condition but filled with love as she regarded her baby sister. Leah wondered at the long, hard internal battle Rachel must have had in deciding not to marry and have children. It was clear she would make a wonderful mother.

She glanced at Edith and saw the woman had dozed off. Tapping Ivan on the arm, she gestured toward his wife. He nodded and tiptoed out of the room, followed by Leah and Sarah. Rachel remained, rocking the baby, though Elizabeth came out, too, and closed the door.

"Aah, the Lord is good," sighed Ivan, sinking into a kitchen chair with a smile on his face. "*Danke*, Elizabeth, for coming so quickly."

"Do you want me to milk the cows?" asked Sarah.

Ivan glanced at the clock. "The time! Yes, child, I could use the help."

"You go. I'll keep watch," said Elizabeth.

"I'll start supper," offered Leah. It pleased her to know her way around the Bylers' kitchen well enough to volunteer for this task alone. Though nothing was said, she sensed approval from the midwife.

The family scattered to the various tasks.

"Would you like some tea?" Leah asked the midwife.

"Ja, danke." The older woman sank into a chair. She smiled. "What a blessing today has been." Her gaze sharpened. "You've never been around a newborn?"

"No. As you know, I'm not Amish. I'm just staying here for a bit." Leah busied herself stoking the stove and pulling out ingredients. "I'm happy to help the Bylers however I can. They've been so good to me."

Elizabeth nodded. "Except for not speaking our language, you could certainly pass for Amish."

Leah was so startled she whirled around in surprise. "Thank you!" she gasped.

"You've a good touch with babies," the midwife continued. "It will be nice for Edith to have an extra pair of hands, though her three girls are so good. *Danke,*" she added as Leah placed a steaming mug before her.

Rachel came out of the bedroom. "Leah, is there any food I could bring *Mamm*? She's hungry."

"Give me five minutes." Leah stirred noodles into the dish Sarah called "dump and go" casserole. When everything was ready, she scooped some food into a bowl and gave it to Rachel on a tray, along with a spoon and napkin.

While Rachel attended her mother, Leah set the table.

Ivan and Sarah came in with foaming buckets of milk, and she helped strain it into jars, then covered the jars with cloths and carried them into the basement so the cream could rise.

And when the time came to bow their heads in silent prayer before the meal, Leah expressed genuine thanks for Edith's safe delivery.

Chapter Fourteen

A week after baby Charity's birth, Isaac waded out among the bean plants in his mother's garden where Leah was picking. "I want to go into Pikeville tomorrow. I have some errands to do. Do you want to come with me? Perhaps you can work on the website you mentioned."

Leah straightened up and smiled. "You changed your mind!"

"*Ja*, I guess." He quirked a smile. "I'm not terribly enthusiastic about the idea, but I suppose it's necessary in this day and age."

"The kind of website I'm thinking of is an information-only website." She dusted her hands on her apron and picked up the basket of beans. "You won't have to do anything with it—you won't have to monitor it in any way—but it will tell customers how best to submit articles or how to subscribe."

"Then *ja*, go ahead."

"I'll start by registering a domain name, then I'll create a website on a free hosting platform. Later I'll go in and link the domain name to the website, and you'll be good to go."

"I didn't understand a word you just said," he admitted. "Here, I'll take that." He relieved her of the basket.

She chuckled. "No worries, this shouldn't be hard to do. I'll make plans to go in with you tomorrow." She visualized the kind of website most suited to his magazine—clean layout, basic design, plain features—and beautiful photos.

"I'll pick you up at the Bylers' then."

In the morning, Leah was ready when Isaac pulled up in the buggy. Edith had given her a list and some money to make some small purchases in town.

"This is a much nicer trip than the last time I was in a buggy." She admired the scenery. "I was so focused on Ivan and his injury I hardly looked around." The clip-clop of the hooves was a soothing rhythm.

"I wanted a car that day since it was an emergency, but I prefer to travel by buggy. It's easier to see things." He waved to a neighbor.

"I can't wait to check the news." Leah nearly quivered with excitement. "I've been out of it for so long—I don't know what's going on in the world."

"Would it make any difference if you did?"

"What do you mean?"

"I mean, you can catch up on all the news, but there isn't much you can do about events taking place in the Middle East or in China or whatever. Sometimes I think it's better not to get too involved in worldly events."

"It's a hard habit to break. When I was a reporter, I spent hours involved in the news each day. It's what I lived for."

"And now?"

Leah looked at the peaceful scenery they passed. "Now…maybe not so much."

"More often than not, the news is bad anyway." Isaac pulled the brim of his hat lower against the sun. "When I was out in the world, I didn't like keeping up with the news. I realized the badness was seeping into my bones, making me a more negative person. It was hard to see *Gott*'s goodness in every person when I was seeing nothing but the bad in people's behaviors. I couldn't handle it."

"The ironic thing is, some might say you were running away, by putting all that behind you."

"For what shall it profit a man, if he shall gain the whole world, and lose his own soul?" quoted Isaac. "I can't save the whole world. That's *Gott*'s job, not mine. My job is to save my own soul, and perhaps influence the souls around me. I'm a simple man, so the only way I could figure out how to save my own soul was to return to my roots."

"I used to think I was obliged to stay up-to-date on everything." Leah sighed. "Not just because of my job, but because it was a moral imperative. Somehow I thought if I reported on the corruption in Washington or the latest terror attack in Europe, I was making a difference. But I can see your point. Maybe I was tearing myself apart, little by little. Then the only way to patch myself together was to develop a thick skin and call it cynicism."

He glanced at her before focusing on the horse. "That's good insight. And I assume you've reported on more than your fair share of bad news?"

"That's an understatement." She sighed and leaned back against the buggy seat. "You might say I was busy reporting on everybody's crooked sticks."

He chuckled. "How's your own stick?" he teased. "Seems to me it's been straightening out."

"I hardly have a choice, do I? It's not like I could get into any trouble out here." Looking out at the landscape as it slowly transitioned from rural to small town, she saw birds, blowing grasses, trees shading the road. "It's going to be hard to leave this all behind."

She felt more than saw him stiffen, though his voice stayed neutral. "It will be hard to imagine you gone."

"Well, I guess there's no rush. I still don't know what I'm going to do."

"Then maybe you could stay here and work on straightening out your stick some more." His smile was back.

"I don't know how much longer I can trespass on the Bylers' hospitality. They've been so good to me. As for my crooked stick, I already said I couldn't get into any trouble out here."

"But a straight stick is more than just avoiding bad behavior. It's about faith."

She felt uncomfortable hearing him talk about his faith. "I'm still working on that."

"*Ja*, it's not something that can be done in a day." He went silent.

She knew by now it wasn't Isaac's nature to push. His restraint made it easier to venture into the subject again. "I wonder," she mused, "how much faith follows actions."

"How do you mean?"

"I mean, as you just said, faith is not something that can be achieved in a day. But what about many days? What about months? If I go through the actions—listening to Ivan read the Bible, praying before meals, attending Sabbath services—all the time being surrounded by people who don't question their faith, how long before it rubs off on me?"

"Who can say? But I think faith seldom comes in a blinding road-to-Damascus flash. It takes time, and it takes practice. And like anything worth mastering—carpentry or sewing or milking a cow or working on a computer—it's something that takes a lot of time and the chance to mess up without fear of someone mocking your efforts. Sometimes it takes patient teachers, and sometimes it's something you wrestle with in private. Everyone's journey is different."

"And did *you* experience this journey?"

"*Ja*, of course. Most of it came after I left and went to college. Before that I never questioned my faith. But college can be challenging. I tried to blend in. I dressed like everyone else, talked like everyone else. I didn't read my Bible, didn't attend Sabbath services. My faith just…slipped away."

"So what happened? When did you realize that?"

"It was just a minor thing, really. I was walking in a park on a Sunday morning. I didn't attend any church… I was just walking. I saw two young girls, maybe ten or eleven years old. They were staring at the smartphones in their hands. They weren't talking to each other, they weren't playing, they were just staring at their phones. And they were dressed badly. Even though they were very young, they were dressed like older teenagers. On a Sunday. I looked at them and I saw my own daughters someday, if I stayed in the *Englisch* world. I compared them to how girls dress here—modestly, in a way pleasing to God. I realized there were too many forces against children, too many things they had to fight off to maintain any measure of goodness."

"So you came back here?"

"Well, it wasn't that fast. But that was the beginning of reaffirming my faith. I wanted a better path, for myself and for my own future children. The only place I knew to get on that path was to come back home. Besides, by then my mother's hip problems were starting to cause her difficulties. My next oldest brother was just about to get married and he wanted to move. That would have left my mother alone. So I came home and became baptized."

"No regrets?"

"None whatever. That doesn't mean I didn't have some periods of adjustment, because I did." He gave a rueful chuckle. "The most ironic thing is, I don't have those mythical daughters yet. Or sons. A man my age often has three or four children already."

"And you want children?"

"*Ja*, of course. They are a legacy, a gift from *Gott*."

That was almost exactly what Ivan had said when Charity was born. "And there's no local woman you're interested in marrying?"

"No, because none are interested in me."

"All because you're tainted by too much time with the English?"

"Maybe a little, but it's also because by the time I came home, all the girls I grew up with were already married, and the ones who aren't married yet think I'm too old. Maybe a young widow will become available." He glanced at her. "Or a visitor."

"Who isn't Amish."

"*Ja*, who isn't Amish."

Pikeville was small, only about twenty-five hundred people, and the library was correspondingly modest. In addition to a parking lot for cars, it also had a long hitching post under the shade of some trees for Amish buggies.

"I'll drop you here while I do my errands." Isaac directed the horse into the parking lot of the small building. "I'm guessing it will take me an hour or so. Will you need more time than that?"

"Yes, but I'll get a good start. I can work on it over several different sessions in town. Can you pick up some lemons and coffee for Edith? Here's the money she gave me."

He handed her down from the buggy. With the physical reserve the Amish normally expressed, the mere act of placing her hand in his was electrifying. Leah sucked in her breath and kept her eyes on the ground.

"In an hour, then." Isaac's voice was gruff.

She looked up in time to see him touch his hat brim before he clucked to the horse and took off. Leah took a deep breath, smoothed down her apron and opened the glass doors of the library building.

Inside, Leah noticed the two librarians engaged in conversation with a patron. No other visitors were present, so she sat down at one of the computers and logged onto the internet. Her first thought was to check the news, but she didn't want to keep Isaac waiting, so she logged onto one of the free website platforms and began building the site for the magazine.

She was so engrossed in her task that it took a few minutes to realize someone was standing behind her. She turned and saw the man who had been talking to the librarians.

"That's not a sight I see every day." He smiled.

"What?"

"An Amish woman using a computer. And one who clearly knows what she's doing too." His gaze flicked to the scar on her cheek.

She felt her face flush. The man wasn't being obnoxious or offensive, but he put her on the defensive. "Is there something I can help you with?"

"No, and I'm sorry to disturb your work. I was just talking with these ladies here about the book sale taking place next week. I'll be putting it in the paper."

"Paper? As in, newspaper?"

"Yes. I work for the *Pikeville Gazette*, so you'll have to excuse my nosiness. It's what makes me a reporter."

"Are you hiring?" she joked.

"What, for the newspaper?"

She nearly clapped a hand over her mouth. "Sorry, that was rude of me…"

"No, no, don't apologize." His eyebrows rose. "Are you interested?"

The thought of reentering the journalism field, however modestly, tugged her. Yet she knew it wasn't safe for a person in witness protection. Warring with herself, she remained silent.

"Seriously, are you interested?" repeated the reporter. "Because if you are, I can almost guarantee my boss would agree. We have a large Amish population around here, so your perspective would be valuable."

"No, really, I can't…" The reluctance in her voice was obvious even to her.

The reporter's eyebrows rose again. "Sounds like you're saying just the opposite—that you're really interested."

"Actually, I am," she confessed, "but it wouldn't work out."

"Then can you tell me how an Amish woman knows her way around a computer as well as you do?"

"No."

"A woman of mystery, eh?" He fished a business card out of a pocket and handed it to her. "I'm Robert Tresedor, by the way. And you are…?"

"Leah. Leah… Byler."

He shook her hand. "I'm sincere. If you're interested in working for us, I think we might be able to accommodate you. And…" At that moment, his cell phone vibrated. He snatched it out of his shirt pocket and looked at the screen. "I'm sorry, I'm expecting a call. Please get in contact with me. Nice to meet you." He walked out of the library, speaking on his phone.

Leah turned back to the computer, her mind buzzing. Okay, so she lied about her last name. But could she work for a small-town newspaper? It would give her a purpose, a direction, while she waited for the criminal investigation in Los Angeles to be concluded, and then she could finally get on with her life.

Her hands rested idle on the keyboard. A part of her knew it was a fool's errand to even think about applying to a small-town paper, yet the lure was there. A job signified independence. Importance. A boost to her confidence.

Yet the logistics were complicated. How would she get to work every day? How could she keep her identity a secret, since she could not allow anyone to verify her identity, much less submit to a background search?

Almost blindly, she resumed work on the website, but the screen blurred and her mind continued to bounce in all directions.

"How's it coming along?"

She nearly shrieked at Isaac's quiet question. "Sorry, you startled me!"

"Wow, you're jumpy." He rested a hand on her shoulder for the briefest moment, then peered at the computer screen. "Is this good? I can't tell."

"I—I didn't get as far along as I hoped." Leah turned to face the computer, anxious to hide her whirlwind thoughts. "I think I'll have to come back another day to work on it some more."

"That's fine. I don't mind getting home sooner anyway. I've got work to do."

"I'll just take a couple minutes to save everything and log off." To her relief, he moved away, allowing her some time to compose her features. She finished on the computer, thanked the librarians and walked with Isaac to the buggy.

On the ride home, Isaac commented about the nature of his errands and anything he noticed in town. "Edith will like the lemons," he chatted. "They were on sale, so I got her an extra amount…"

Leah stayed mostly silent. Her mind ran with meeting the reporter, and she didn't feel like prattling about lemons.

"You seem awfully quiet," he finally observed as they neared the Bylers' farm. "Too much bad news on the internet?"

"Actually, I didn't even check the news." Leah pinched the bridge of her nose. "Isaac, I met someone while you were off doing errands. I'm—I'm not sure what you'll think of it."

"Oh?"

"He's a reporter for the local newspaper, and he more or less invited me to apply for a job."

"What?" He gaped at her.

"Yes. He noticed me working on the computer and said it wasn't a common sight, to see an Amish woman on a computer."

"And based on that, he offered you a job?"

"Well, not exactly. When he explained he was a reporter, I jokingly asked if the newspaper was hiring, and that's how the whole subject came up."

"But you refused him, of course." His lips compressed. At her silence, he looked at her. "You *didn't* refuse him?"

"I didn't commit myself in any way, of course, but I didn't outright refuse him either. He gave me his business card and asked me to get in contact with him."

"Leah, you can't do this."

She bristled. She hadn't risen in the competitive ranks of journalism to be told she "couldn't" do something. "Why not?" she snapped. "I'm in limbo here until…" She trailed off. She'd forgotten Isaac didn't know she was in witness protection—which made his opposition even more high-handed.

He glanced at her sharply. "Until what?"

"Nothing."

"That's not true and you know it. What's the real reason you want to work for this newspaper?"

"It would give me back some semblance of the life I had before my accident. Plus it would be a boost to my confidence."

"So in other words, it boils down to your pride and your ego. That's not the Amish way."

"That's not fair! Journalism is my profession! My passion!"

"So it is." He stared straight ahead. "Sometimes I forget you're not one of us."

That comment hurt more than Leah wanted to admit. She'd grown so comfortable in an Amish *kapp* that she, too, sometimes forgot she wasn't part of the community. "Why are you so angry? You know I'm not Amish."

"I think I'm angrier at myself than anything. Or maybe *disillusioned* is the word. But this just illustrates the gulf between us, the contrast to being *of* the world, but not *in* the world. You still want to go back to what you came from, your career and your life among the *Englisch*. I can't blame you. But I blame myself for..." He huffed in frustration, then fell silent.

Blame himself for what? Deep within, she knew the answer.

"You and the Bylers have helped me get back on my feet." Leah spoke with dignity. "Maybe it's time I started thinking about my future."

"And maybe it's time to nail my head on straight," he

muttered. He pulled the horse to a stop in front of the Bylers' farm. "Don't forget Edith's lemons and coffee."

Stung at his abrupt coldness, Leah climbed out from the buggy clutching the groceries. With a flick of his hat brim, he drove away.

Leah stared after him. The weight of his disapproval felt like a sack of cement on her shoulders. She realized she now faced a complication she hadn't anticipated.

She was in love with Isaac.

Chapter Fifteen

"You can't be serious," Edith said, holding baby Charity in her arms. "You can't work at a newspaper. You're in hiding, remember?"

"I know." Leah ran a hand over her face. "It was an impulsive thing to say to the reporter, but I confess I've been fantasizing about actually doing it."

"But why? You seem so happy and content, toggling back and forth between the Sommers and here. Why would you suddenly want to work for a newspaper?"

"Isaac asked me whether it was just a matter of pride and ego."

"Is it?"

"Maybe." Leah snapped another clean, dry diaper and folded it, laying it on a stack on the kitchen table. The house was quiet, and she was alone with Edith and knew it was a good time to bring up her troubles. "But, Edith, there's something more. Isaac was very unhappy when I suggested the possibility. *Disillusioned*, that's the word he used. He said it illustrates the gulf between us, the contrast to being *of* the world but not *in* the world."

"What are your feelings for Isaac?"

The Amish weren't big on discussing feelings, Leah knew by now, so Edith's question meant the answer was important. "I'm in love with him," she admitted.

"That's what I thought. You're aware of the problems?"

"Of course. I've had warnings from Sarah and Rachel not to toy with his affections. It's just that—well, we have a lot in common and are very compatible in so many ways."

"Except one."

"Right, except one. Faith. He left the community once. And then he came back."

"He did more than come back. He came back and was baptized. That's a commitment every bit as serious as a marriage vow."

"I know that now. Maybe that's why I thought about taking up this reporter on the chance of a job. It would give me independence and put some distance between Isaac and me."

"Are you that anxious to leave us?"

Leah looked up. Edith's eyes were soft and kindly. "I would have thought you'd be anxious to get rid of me," she said slowly. "I've been troubling you all summer, plaguing you with my ignorance."

"But you didn't stay ignorant. Now that the children are in school again, I've come to depend on you more and more. Sarah is helping Ivan in the shop and with the livestock since the boys are in school, and she'll be married in November anyway. Rachel is student teaching, so with the *kinner* gone, I'll admit you've been a blessing. I don't know what I'd have done without you."

"You'd have hired someone to help you, as you said you did when your last baby was born."

"*Ja*, so this all works out. It's a *Gott* thing."

"A God thing," echoed Leah. She dropped into the chair opposite Edith. "You know, I've been realizing something a little scary—I'm feeling more fulfilled here than I did when I was working. As a journalist, I constantly chased after the next hot news story. It never ended. There was always another news story to chase. But now..." She fell silent.

"But now...?" Edith prompted.

"I don't know. I'm different. It's not just the lack of modern conveniences. It's not just the sense of community. It's other things too. The way Ivan reads the Bible in the evenings. The Sabbath services. The way everyone I meet is humble and not competitive. The... the faith."

"And you feel like something is different inside?"

"Yes. And I don't know what to make of it. Maybe it's... I don't know."

"Maybe it's that *Gott*-shaped hole in your heart," Edith suggested gently. "Maybe it's starting to be filled. Have you thought about that?" She lifted the infant onto her shoulder, patting.

"Reluctantly, yes."

"Why reluctantly?"

Leah gave a somber smile. "You've never felt any doubts about your faith, have you?"

"No, of course not."

"Then you can't understand what it's like to have no

faith at all. To discover that God might really care about me is a little frightening. It's like—like I'd lose control of my own fate, my own destiny."

"But why is that a bad thing?"

"I don't know that it is. It's just scary."

"Seems like *Gott* directed you here. Maybe it was time to reevaluate your life."

"I've been thinking the same thing." Leah smoothed another diaper. "I spent so many years working in a high-stress atmosphere that I'd forgotten what it's like not to be competitive. My friends were the same way. We were all striving and jostling and comparing each other's careers. But no matter how much I acquired or succeeded, something was always missing. It was like I was swimming with sharks and telling myself swimming with sharks was normal."

"So you don't miss that competitiveness?"

"No. On the contrary, not being immersed in it makes me realize how selfish and greedy I'd been— not so much for *things* as for fame and recognition. I was trying to fill something up inside me. Yet that impulse still raises its head sometimes. Want to hear something embarrassing?"

Edith nodded.

"When I first got here, and the first time I sat in on the Bible readings with you as a family, I couldn't follow Ivan's German." Leah kept her eyes on the growing pile of diapers. "So my mind wandered and I started looking at the children, and how respectfully they behaved during the reading. The journalist in me started thinking what it would be like to write about how you raise and train children. Then I started thinking about *this* I could write about, and *that* I could write about, and my mind was just buzzing. When Ivan finished reading, I was a little ashamed to be thinking about my career during a time when I should be concentrating on the word of God."

"Perhaps you should think about it in a different way," suggested Edith. "Perhaps *Gott* was talking to you about ways to leave behind your old life and embrace a new one."

"The thought occurred to me too." Leah sighed. "There's so much to think about."

"It reminds me of something I once read," commented Edith. "All the bad stuff people deal with— money, poverty, ambition, war, empires, slavery—all these things are just the terrible story of man trying to find something other than *Gott* which will make him happy."

Leah went very still. She thought of her career, her ambition, even the depression from her scarred face— was all this merely something that she was grasping at, trying to make herself happy?

She dropped into a chair and stared unseeing at the floor. Had God put her here for a reason? Was He trying to tell her something? Was He doing His best to make her, Leah, happy?

She found her eyes were swimming with tears. She raised her face and looked at Edith, whose own eyes were soft with compassion. "Are you happy, child?" Edith asked softly.

"No." The word was ragged. Leah broke down crying, the ugly hiccupping sobs that she knew would leave her face blotched and red. But she didn't care.

She wept from a sudden realization: she *did* have a God-shaped hole in her heart, and she'd spent her whole life chasing after things she hoped would fill it. Education, career, ambition, accolades, pride, ego. When it was all snatched away from her that night in the alley, when the gang member had slashed her face, she thought she'd lost everything.

But now she was beginning to realize it wasn't an ending—it was a beginning. Here in this plain kitchen, next to a woman who'd just experienced for the seventh time the miracle of birth—all of this was directing her toward one unavoidable fact: God *did* love her. And He was the only one capable of bringing her happiness.

Edith made no move to comfort Leah but merely removed a clean handkerchief from her apron pocket and pushed it across the table toward her. Then she rocked with the baby across her shoulder.

"I'm sorry," sniffed Leah after a few minutes. "I don't know what came over me." She mopped her face and blew her nose.

"It's a powerful thing, isn't it, to know *Gott* watches out for us," commented Edith. "Don't be ashamed to cry, child. We're only human."

Leah gave a hiccupping sigh and slumped in her chair. "I—I just realized that maybe God was guiding me here the whole time. I've been happier here than I have at any other time in my life—and that makes no sense to someone raised as I was, to believe a career is paramount and family life is just an afterthought."

"I know it's hard, going against early training."

She wiped her eyes with the handkerchief, feeling drained. "It's funny, during my first week here, Rachel and I were out weeding the garden one day. I mentioned how angry I was about getting my face cut up. That's the first time I heard about the so-called God-shaped hole, when Rachel brought it up. And for a moment, I felt this extraordinary feeling. It was, well, like a wave washed over me. It felt cleansing, like it might wash away my anger and bitterness and leave peace behind. Then it faded, and I didn't give it any more thought, until now. Now I remember that feeling of peace. It's— it's back. I guess it took a disfigurement on my face to get my head clear."

"I think your disfigurement is much less than you think," replied Edith. "I never see your scar now."

"Just like I never see Rachel's small size. We talked about that not long after I got here. She said the Amish look much more closely at what someone looks like on the inside than on the outside."

"Rachel is my wisdom child." Edith smiled. "She's wise beyond her years. It was hard for her at first, accepting her condition and deciding never to marry. But she's adjusted and is now in a position to help others whenever they need some of that wisdom. She's a natural leader too—she'll make an excellent schoolteacher."

"I could learn a lot from her," Leah said.

The next morning, she opened her dresser drawer and pulled out the crooked stick she had stepped on early in the summer. She sat down on the bed and stared at it.

Had God sent her here to straighten out her stick? The witness protection program could have placed her anywhere, but it placed her here, among people who didn't see her scarred face and who—in their gentle, unassuming way—had spent the last few months laying their straight sticks next to her crooked one. Now, at least, she understood that. She realized one of the most powerful tools of a religious life was straightening one's stick—walking the straight and narrow.

She took Robert Tresedor's business card and tossed it in the woodstove.

Then she went to visit Isaac.

"You threw the card away!" Isaac straightened up from riveting some leather in his workshop.

"I did more than that. I burned it in the woodstove." Leah fiddled with a scrap of leather.

"Why?"

She met his gaze. "Because your opinion mattered more than my ego. Or my pride."

He closed his eyes and pinched the bridge of his nose. "Praise *Gott*," he murmured.

"There's more. I don't know how to explain it, but I'll try."

"Does it have to do with the newspaper job?"

"No. Yes. Kinda." Leah dropped onto a stool and felt her eyes prickle with some of the emotion she felt the day before. "I was talking things over with Edith, trying to wrestle with my confusion and, as you called it, my pride and ego. It's like I couldn't let it go. And… and…and I burst out crying because I realized everything I did, I did because I was trying to find happiness without God."

His hands remained idle. "And what did you conclude?"

"That I was wrong and God was right." She sniffed

and groped in her pocket for the handkerchief she'd learned to carry. She wiped her eyes. "I think I understand now. Suddenly the offer from the reporter didn't hold my interest anymore. So I burned his business card. It felt like a huge weight had been lifted off my shoulders. Not the business card, the realization about God."

A few moments passed in emotional silence. Then she raised her head and saw Isaac's eyes were closed and his lips moved silently. Then he opened his eyes—and smiled. "My prayers," he said softly, "are answered."

She gave a shaky laugh. "Mine too."

But it wasn't entirely true. She didn't know what to do about being in love with Isaac.

Chapter Sixteen

But the next day, her newfound joy was shattered.

"You got a letter." Edith pointed to an envelope on the kitchen table.

Leah froze. "Who from?" No one was supposed to know where she was.

"The return address says it's the US Marshals Service."

That was the organization that had placed her in the witness protection program. Leah's heart started pounding.

"Here." Edith thrust the letter into her hand. "You'd best read it alone. Go upstairs."

She nodded and groped her way out of the kitchen and up the stairs to her bedroom. Whatever the letter said, she would need time to compose herself after reading it.

She closed the door behind her and dropped into the rocking chair. She tried to pray, but no words came. With shaking fingers, she tore open the envelope.

The news was worse than she thought. The letter

informed her that "the threats to her life are not likely to decrease at any time," given the coordinated nature of gang connections across the country as well as her "public identity as an investigative reporter." She was advised to "adopt a new identity on a permanent basis" rather than risk returning to California, much less television.

She dropped the letter into her lap and stared at it, unseeing.

This changed things. This changed everything. Everything she had lived for, worked for, gone to school for…gone. Forever. Even her name was no longer safe to use.

She leaned her head against the rocker, and tears came to her eyes. What was she going to do? This question had haunted her on and off since arriving here, but this clinched her fate. She had to completely reinvent herself. But how?

Suddenly this placement—living anonymously among the Amish—seemed less like a refuge and more like a prison, all due to circumstances beyond her control. While she could leave anytime, she didn't know where to go or what to do to earn a living.

She tried to pray. Tried to lay her troubles in the lap of God, as Rachel had suggested, but the words would not come. She felt adrift, rootless, purposeless…

She read the letter again. It listed assistance she could get—legally changing her name and social security number, remedial training for a different line of work—but it was all too much to take in.

Heavyhearted, she descended the stairs, knowing Edith was curious about the contents of the letter.

"Bad news?"

"Yes." Leah dropped into a chair and nodded thanks as Edith pushed a cup of tea toward her. "I can't return to my old life. They suggest I adopt a completely new identity." She drew a ragged breath. "Oh, Edith, what am I going to do?"

"Nothing yet," said the older woman. "You're in too much shock to make a sound decision. Just think on it for a week or two. The Lord will provide an answer."

Leah bit back a sarcastic retort. Edith's complete faith and dependence on God's will seemed out of place in light of this new crisis. To just...*do nothing* seemed like a cop-out.

Yet she had no choice. She could rail against fate, bang her head against a metaphorical brick wall, scream and cry her distress...or she could wait and think on it for a week or two.

Who knew. Maybe God *would* provide an answer.

And what about Isaac? She had a sudden urge to discuss the matter with him. There were strong feelings between them, and he had the right to know the true reason she was here. It was time to clear the air and lay the matter at his feet.

"I have to talk to Isaac. He doesn't know I'm in witness protection, and this complicates things."

"I thought you might." Edith dropped a hand onto Leah's shoulder. "Go do it now."

Draining her tea and dragging her steps, she set out on the now familiar road to the Sommers'.

Isaac was in his workshop. Leah bypassed her usual knock at the front door and her daily chat with Eleanor to tackle the man directly. "Good afternoon, Isaac."

He looked up and smiled. "Hello!"

"Can I talk to you for a minute?"

His expression changed as he examined her face. "*Ja.* In here, or elsewhere?"

"Here is as good a place as any."

He gestured toward a stool near a worktable. She seated herself while he leaned against a bench. "What's wrong?"

"I got some bad news today, but before I go into it, I need to tell you something about my background, and why I'm here. There…there are some things about me you don't know."

His expression became wary. "You said you were recovering from a car accident."

"That was a lie, and I hope you'll forgive me and understand why it was necessary." She took a breath. "It's true that I was an investigative journalist, and my career ended when I got this scar." She touched her cheek. "But I didn't get the scar from a car accident. I was reporting on some gang violence in Los Angeles and witnessed a brutal double murder."

He sucked in his breath.

She nodded at his expression. "My cameraman caught it on film. What happened then…the murderers saw us and came after us. One of them tackled me and started carving up my face before Ted—my cameraman—kicked him off and dragged me away. He saved my life. Took me straight to the hospital. I was there for a long time, healing, and then they had to do reconstruction work. While I was in the hospital, some of the gang members nearly broke into my room. They knew who I was, where I lived, everything. So—I was sent into witness protection. I've been in hiding all these months I've been here."

He stared at her. "You're kidding."

"I wish I were, but no."

He drew a ragged breath. "You suddenly got a lot more complicated than I expected."

"It gets worse. I got a letter today from the US Marshals Service informing me that it's too dangerous to resume my former life or identity in any way—they recommend I adopt a completely new identity." She stared at the floor, her eyes prickling. "I don't know what to do now. My life…" Tears leaked out of her eyes.

In two steps he reached her, pressed her head against his chest, and she burst out sobbing.

"I don't know what to do, where to go…" she hiccupped, grateful for his strong arms around her.

In a few moments the storm passed, and he fished out a bandana and handed it to her. "It's clean," he clarified.

She nodded and mopped her face. "Sorry," she mumbled.

"For what, being human?" He retreated to his former position by the workbench. "You obviously have a lot to think about right now."

"Yeah." Her shoulders slumped. "It's so strange. A year ago, I thought I was on top of the world. I had a stellar career, receiving journalism awards. People recognized me on the streets and would stop to shake my hand. I made a great salary and had a beautiful apartment. I had a nice car. Then, with the slash of a knife, it was all taken away."

"Depends on what you mean by 'taken away.'" Isaac toyed with a piece of leather harness. "Sure, you lost your career and your salary. Presumably you still have your apartment and its contents, and your car, items that you can sell for money. But no question, those were big blows. However, there's an old expression that seems apt here—'When *Gott* closes a door, He opens a window.' You may not be able to resume your old life, but there's a kind of excitement in the thought of creating a new one."

Leah lifted her head and hiccupped. "Excitement? What do you mean?"

"I mean, you have a clean slate. You can take a new name, you can take a new background if you want. You can…" He paused. "Straighten your stick."

She jerked. "Straighten my stick…" It was only the previous day she had looked at that crooked stick residing in her dresser drawer. Was it straightening out? Here Isaac was saying this was her golden opportunity.

"How do I do it?" she wondered. "How can I reinvent myself and straighten my stick?"

"It seems to me you already have. You're here, you're adapting very well and you're becoming a valuable member of the community. You've been living a fairly 'straight stick' life for the last few months. You even have a new career ahead of you—writing. You're already writing for me, and as I've said, you should write a book too. Under a new name, of course."

"But that brings me back to the obstacle I mentioned before—I'm not Amish."

"Ah. Yes." Isaac looked down at the floor. "And that might prove insurmountable."

* * *

By the next day, the Bylers had all heard the news, but they didn't bring up the topic very much—at least, not in her presence. It was not the Amish way to push.

Rachel joined her to work in the Sommers' garden. Leah welcomed her company—the young woman's wisdom was something that might help pierce the fog of helplessness Leah felt.

Isaac wasn't home. "Out interviewing someone in Pikeville," explained Eleanor.

"We'll strip the last of the pea vines," said Rachel. "It shouldn't take long."

"Here are the baskets." Eleanor pointed to some containers.

"For a woman who can't get around very well, Eleanor sure works hard," commented Leah as they waded into the rows of peas. "I'll bet dollars to doughnuts she's already processed all the beans Isaac and I picked yesterday."

"It wouldn't surprise me." Rachel reached for a vine and started stripping off pods, her movements quick and efficient. "I'm glad you were able to get this garden back in shape and producing again. Though that said, since it's just feeding her and Isaac, they don't need as much. Plus of course her other children share their produce with her."

Leah was silent for a few moments. "Rachel, can I ask you something?"

"Of course."

"What would it take to convert and become Amish?"

Rachel paused and looked at Leah. Then she straightened up and leaned against one of the pea stakes. "Are you serious?"

"Yes. It's been on my mind for quite a while now, and I figure a thought that won't let go is something I should pay attention to."

Rachel nodded. "That's too big a question for me. I think you should go talk to Daniel Stoltzfus, the bishop."

Leah experienced a quiver. "He seems like such an intimidating man."

"He's very kind, but he's also the person who is better able to discern if you're serious."

"How do I talk to him?"

"After Sabbath services. Ask him if you can come over to speak with him during the week."

"That leaves me two days to gather up my courage."

The short woman smiled. "Don't make him out to be that bad."

"Except potentially he holds my future in his hands."

Rachel nodded. "Okay, I can see that. I'll go with you when you ask to meet with him, if that will help your courage." She resumed picking. "Why the interest, though? Most *Englisch* find they can't give up modern conveniences and such."

Leah also resumed her work. "It has a lot to do with yesterday's letter. I don't know what to do with myself now, at least professionally."

"Just a warning, that's not a good enough reason to become Amish. A conversion like that wouldn't last."

"I know. I don't want to make any decision on the rebound, so to speak. But I think it's deeper than that. I've spent my whole professional life dealing with drama and excitement, reporting the news. I've never *not* been steeped in it before. It surprises me how little I miss it, how my body is responding to the lack of stress. I feel better, stronger. I like the challenge of tackling projects, like this garden." She let go of some pea pods long enough to gesture. "I told your mother how much I liked the idea of taking over this garden and seeing what I can do."

"You've done well," approved Rachel. "And I'll admit, you're different from every other *Englisch* I've ever met. *Ja*, talk to the bishop after the service."

Throughout the Sabbath service, Leah found her heart beating fast whenever she thought about talking to Bishop Stoltzfus. The service couldn't be hurried, of course, and at any rate she couldn't speak with him alone until after the post-service meal.

Though men and women alike avoided looking across the room at one another during the service—each was sunk in his or her private thoughts and prayer—she glanced at the bishop. He was a tall and spare man, with a wispy gray beard and stooped shoulders. Yet he carried an air of power and quiet authority.

"Nervous?" whispered Rachel when at last the women sat down to eat afterward.

"Yes," she whispered back. "I hope I'm doing the right thing."

"If you're serious about converting, this is the first step."

She nodded and took a deep breath. Another challenge.

Shortly before the Bylers departed to return home after the meal, Leah walked with Rachel toward Bishop

Stoltzfus, who was talking with a group of elders near some buggies. "Bishop Stoltzfus, may I speak with you?" asked Rachel.

The older man lifted his eyebrows but nodded and stepped away.

"You know Leah Porte, who's been staying with us," said Rachel. "She would like to speak with you privately sometime this week. I'll let you explain," added Rachel to Leah. "Excuse me." And she walked away.

Left alone with the bishop, Leah wiped her sweaty hands on her apron. "I—I'd like to ask you some questions," she began. "But not here. In private. Would sometime this week work?"

"*Ja.* Why don't you come over tomorrow? Bring Rachel for propriety's sake. Eleven o'clock?"

"Yes, thank you." Leah backed away. "Thank you." She turned and fled.

"I don't know why he makes me so nervous," she babbled to Rachel after locating her in the kitchen. "We're meeting tomorrow morning at eleven. He said to bring you along for propriety's sake."

"*Ja*, it's normal for a man in a position of authority not to be alone with any woman he's not related to." Rachel nodded. "I'll come."

For the rest of the afternoon Leah wondered just how to broach the subject to Bishop Stoltzfus. In the end she decided on bluntness. How else could it be?

She slept badly that night. In the morning Rachel offered to accompany her to the Sommers', where she explained to Eleanor that they had an appointment with the bishop later in the morning and so wouldn't be able to stay long. Eleanor nodded but didn't inquire.

"This way *Mamm* won't know you've been to see the bishop," explained Rachel as they set off for the Stoltzfus' farm some distance away. "I figure this is your business and not everyone else needs to know about it."

"Thank you. I didn't sleep well last night for thinking about it."

"What inspired you to think about converting to begin with?"

"I don't know. All I can say is, it's an idea that's been growing and I can't seem to shake it."

"Don't be surprised if Bishop Stoltzfus is discouraging," warned Rachel. "It's unusual for an *Englisch* to convert to Amish. Or more truthfully, to *remain* Amish."

"I'm aware of that. Believe me, I'm aware of that. But I want to ask anyway."

Bishop Stoltzfus's farm, explained Rachel as they approached the handsome white structure, was now run by his son. The bishop and his wife lived in the *daadi haus* around back. Rachel walked behind and knocked on the door of the home extension.

"Good morning," said Rachel when that good lady opened the door. "We're here to see Bishop Stoltzfus."

"*Ja*, come in."

The older woman led the way into a study, plainly furnished with a desk, several chairs, a bookshelf and nothing else. Bishop Stoltzfus was writing something.

"Good morning." The bishop rose. "Rachel, do you want to stay, or would it be better to visit with my wife?"

Rachel looked at Leah. "Which would you prefer?"

"Go ahead and visit. I'll be fine."

Rachel nodded and slipped out the door, closing it behind her.

"Please, sit," said Bishop Stoltzfus, indicating a chair. "How can I help you?"

"As you know," began Leah, "I've been with the Bylers since early June. Do you know the circumstances under which I came here?"

"*Ja*, of course," said the bishop. "It was my influence that settled you here, in fact. I have *Englisch* relatives in law enforcement, and they contacted me about your case. Ivan volunteered to hide you as long as necessary. But not many others know, only a few of the elders. Everyone else believes you're recovering from a car accident."

"That's right. I'm very grateful you placed me here. But—but something just happened. I received this." She took the letter from her pocket and pushed it across the desk to him. "It basically says I cannot return to my old life, ever, and recommends I adopt a new identity."

"May I read it?"

"Of course."

The bishop unfolded the paper and read it. Then he refolded it and handed it back. "And what is your reaction to this?"

"I was pretty upset, as you can imagine. I knew my career was over when I got this." She touched her scar. "But I had vague hopes I could resume working as a journalist—maybe not in Los Angeles, but elsewhere. Now my options are more limited. Or at least, my future must change."

He nodded. "And how may I help you today? Is there something I can do to assist in your new identity?"

"No. I wanted to ask you a completely different question, but I hope your answer won't be influenced by that letter. It was just to let you know what I'm facing. The question I wanted to ask you is this—what would it take for me to convert and become Amish?"

Evidently this came as a surprise to the good bishop, for she saw his eyes widen before he leaned back in his chair and steepled his fingers. "I didn't expect that," he admitted. "And it's a most unusual request."

"I know. Believe me, I know." She scrubbed a hand over her face. "But you know how it is when a thought won't leave you alone? I keep wondering if I'm being pushed to ask this."

"Pushed in what way?"

"Pushed by God, perhaps? Who knows."

"Miss Porte…" Bishop Stoltzfus leaned forward and folded his arms on the desk. "Yours is not the first request I've received from an *Englischer* who is interested in joining us. But you're something of an unusual case, being as you're living as one of us and, I might add, blending in very well. I've heard nothing negative about you."

She jerked her head up. Compliments among the Amish were so rare that to hear one always came as a surprise.

He held up a hand, then dropped it again. "But that doesn't mean we let just anyone stay," he continued. "Most of the *Englisch* who ask me about becoming Amish try to claim they were born in the wrong century, and make it sound as if they would have no problems giving up modern conveniences. All they see is—" he paused as if searching for the right words "—is the off-grid lifestyle and quaint clothing. They don't understand the lifestyle and clothing are just outer manifestations of the inner life."

"I'm aware of that." Leah decided to be honest. "And that's why I'm here today. The off-grid lifestyle, as you call it, takes some getting used to, but thanks to the Bylers' help I'm getting the hang of things. But that's not what's bugging me. I keep feeling…*pushed.* I have no other way to describe it."

"Miss Porte, may I ask you what religion you were before coming here?"

"That's just it. I *wasn't* religious. I won't say I was an atheist, so I guess you'd call it agnostic. I just never gave much thought to God one way or the other. But every night, Ivan gathers his family around and reads a chapter or two of the Bible. It was too hard for me to follow in German, so Edith gave me an English Bible I could follow. Then I started reading it. Then I started attending Sabbath services. Then…then I started to pray. And believe me, Mr. Stoltzfus, it sounds like a foreign language just for me to admit that."

He nodded. "It's not often I've come across anyone who says it's the spiritual side that attracts them. Are you truly certain that's your pull?"

"No. I'm not. And I know I can't expect a yes-or-no answer from you today. I just wanted to lay things before you—that was Rachel's suggestion, by the way—and ask about the possibility."

"Now let me ask something else. How does Isaac Sommer fit into all this?"

She clasped her hands. "I won't deny he's interested in me, but he's fully aware of his position as a baptized member of this community, and equally aware I'm not. I find him a fascinating man. We've worked together on the magazine, as you know. Since I'm more familiar with computer programs than he is, I volunteered to do some of the computer work. But Rachel warned me early on he was in courting mode, which he's admitted. I haven't encouraged him because I know what could happen to him if I did."

The bishop nodded. "That was wise. I won't deny there are many obstacles to you joining us. As you can imagine, converts are rare…but not unknown. Unfortunately the percentage of converts who relapse and return to the wider world is fairly significant. But one thing is for certain—converts who don't have the spiritual interest don't last."

"That makes sense."

"The Amish emphasize three things in their communities," the bishop continued. "Those are the values of unity, humility and submission. For outsiders to comply with these principles is often difficult. But," he added, adopting a stern expression once again, "not many people can pass the test of time, so to speak. If you're serious about becoming Amish, I recommend a few things. First, you must learn *Deitsch*."

She nodded. "I know a little bit of High German from my school days—that's one of the reasons I was placed here for protection, as opposed to anywhere else—but I haven't tried to pick up the Pennsylvania Dutch dialect. I'll try harder."

"Next, you should become familiar with the *Ordnung*."

"Is there a book I could study?"

"No, ironically there isn't. It's an unwritten code. The purpose is to uphold and unify us as a community. You might say adherence to the rules of the *Ordnung* is one test of membership. At one level, we feel a community without rules—that anyone can enter or leave as they please—is hardly worth being part of."

Leah nodded. "I can understand that."

"*Gut*. You'll find, however, the *Ordnung* serves a deeper purpose, as well. We feel these rules are based on the Bible, and they help church members live better Christian lives. The strictures of the *Ordnung* aren't found in the Bible, but they're based on biblical principles. It outlines not just what technology we deem acceptable, but it also determines matters of dress, expressions of pride or envy, things like that."

Leah touched her *kapp*. "Such as covering the hair."

Bishop Stoltzfus smiled. "Yes, though that *is* found in Scripture. But by submitting oneself to the *Ordnung*, it demonstrates a humble spirit. We all have to bury individualism and arrogance for the good of the community. And that," he concluded, "is probably one of the most difficult things for an *Englischer* to accept and follow."

"You don't sound very optimistic about my chances." Leah spoke with a touch of asperity.

"I mean no offense, of course. Of the few who convert, only about one-third remain Amish. The other two-thirds leave after a while. It's simply too difficult for outsiders to accept and live by our rules."

"Is there hope for me?"

"There's always hope. But you've been with us a relatively short time—just four months. Since you arrived at the Bylers', you've slipped into our ways with astonishing speed. I confess it's unusual. But it's not enough. You'll have to remain with us, learning our ways, for a long time. Then all members of our church would need to be in favor of your candidacy. If all goes well, then you'll take instructional classes for many months. This all happens before you can be baptized."

She nodded. "I can understand the challenges. It will take time to see if I'll fit."

"*Ja.* One of the problems we experience is outsiders tend to romanticize our way of life. We're seen as throwbacks to a happier time when people lived in harmony with each other, with *Gott*, with the earth. Those who seek us based on those terms don't last, because *Gott* isn't the center of their lives. But *Gott* is the center of *our* lives. One of the reasons we do adult baptism is because it's critical our members understand the seriousness of their commitment, something children can't do. It is far better not to make a vow than to make a vow and later break it. That's why we take both baptism and marriage seriously. There is no going back."

She raised her chin. "You may be right. I might find it too difficult. But do I have permission to try?"

"Of course." He smiled. "You've been a huge blessing to Ivan and Edith, especially since Edith's last baby was born. They speak highly of you. One of the things you'll have to determine is whether they will keep you living in their home for the long term. The witness protection was meant to be a short-term commitment. They may need the room in their house. If that's the case, we can find somewhere else where you can stay."

Leah fiddled with her apron. "I've been doing a lot

of work at Isaac's, since his mother is not as mobile as she used to be. Eleanor and I get along very well. Would it be inappropriate for me to stay there?"

"*Ja*, it would be inappropriate. For an unmarried couple to be in the same house—especially since Isaac has expressed interest in you—would cause tongues to wag. Remember, your acceptance among us must be universal or it could sow dissent."

"I understand." She sighed. "Thank you for your time today, Bishop. This is what I needed to hear. And for the time being, I'll stay with the Bylers, unless they'd rather I find somewhere else to go."

Chapter Seventeen

"How'd it go?" asked Rachel on the walk home.

"About what I expected. He told me a little of what I need to do, notably learn *Deitsch* and abide by the *Ordnung*. But if I do stay and convert, he wasn't overly optimistic about the likelihood of my remaining Amish."

Rachel chuckled. "I'll tell you one thing—I wouldn't be surprised if you became baptized after all."

"I appreciate the vote of confidence."

"What are you going to tell Isaac?"

"Just what I've told you. I already let him know the truth about why I landed here to begin with. Now I'll let him know about my discussion with Bishop Stoltzfus." She paused, then added, "He deserves to know."

Rachel nodded. "That's wise. In fact, why don't you go talk with him now? I'll just head home. It's late enough you'll probably stay for supper. I'll let *Mamm* know."

"I'll do that. And Rachel..." Leah stopped in the road and bent down to hug her. "Thank you. For everything. You've helped me more than you'll ever know."

She thought she saw a sparkle of moisture in the young woman's eyes as she returned the hug. Then she turned and walked away.

Leah headed for the Sommers' home. It was close to dinner, and as she suspected, both Eleanor and Isaac were in the kitchen.

"Leah!" exclaimed Eleanor as she answered the door. "You're a mite late, child, but won't you stay for dinner?"

"I will, if you don't mind." Leah toyed with the idea of asking to speak to Isaac alone, then changed her mind. If she and Isaac were to have a future together, it would involve his mother, as well. She needed the older woman's blessing.

With the meal on the table, she bowed her head and asked God not just for a blessing on the food but also for a blessing on her future.

"What have you been doing today?" began Isaac, reaching for a platter and scooping some food onto his plate.

"I had an appointment I wanted to tell you both about." Leah toyed with her fork. "It was with Bishop Stoltzfus."

Isaac froze. Eleanor paused.

"I went to ask him a very important question— namely, what it would take for me to convert and become Amish."

"And…" The word came out as a croak. Isaac cleared his throat and tried again. "And what did he say?"

"He gave me every warning under the sun but summed it up by saying I was welcome to try. He said I'd need to learn Pennsylvania Dutch and become familiar with and abide by the *Ordnung*. We had quite a lengthy discussion. He suggested it might take as long as a couple of years, all told." She looked at her plate.

"Child, that was a brave thing to do," said Eleanor, her eyes sparkling with moisture.

"I was scared," she admitted. "The bishop is an intimidating fellow. But he was fair and honest—both about my chances, and about the likelihood of a conversion being a lasting state of affairs."

"Will Ivan and Edith let you continue to stay with them?" asked Eleanor.

"I don't know. I'll ask them tonight. I'll confess I asked about the possibility of rooming here, but Bishop Stoltzfus said it would not reflect well on me."

"Of course not." Eleanor seemed to grasp the implications at once.

Isaac was silent through this exchange. Not wanting to make any assumptions and look like a fool, she only said to him, "So it looks like I'll be able to work on the magazine for the foreseeable future."

Isaac abruptly shoved his chair back and stood up. "Excuse me, please." He strode out of the kitchen door toward the back of the house.

Stricken, Leah stared after him. "What did I say?" she whispered.

Eleanor smiled, and her lips trembled. "I think he's overwhelmed at the thought you might stay. He hasn't said much to me, but it's plain as day he has feelings for you."

Leah bit her lip. "The feeling's mutual."

"Go after him, child. You need to talk."

She nodded, snatched the napkin off her lap and went outside.

Isaac was standing in the shade of a tree, resting his hand on the trunk and breathing as if he'd been running.

"Isaac? What's wrong?"

"Nothing."

"That's a lie and you know it." She picked her way over some gravel toward the tree. "Tell me…"

The words ended on a gasp, because he turned and grabbed her, enveloping her in a hard embrace and burying his face in her neck. She felt him shaking.

"I can't believe you did that," he whispered against her *kapp*. "I can't believe there's a chance you could stay here among us, always. I can't believe it."

Except for when she'd wept against his chest, it was the first time he'd held her. The Amish reserve against physical affection was so ingrained that to be hugged this hard illustrated how powerful was the emotion behind it.

She felt tears prickle her eyes. "It hasn't happened yet. There's a lot ahead of me. Possibly years. The bishop said the decision would have to be unanimous among the church members. And I'll have to be baptized."

He drew a shuddering breath and released her, shoving his hands into his pockets. He turned to look at the western sky. "But there's hope."

"Yes, there's hope. It's not just you, Isaac. It's not you alone that's luring me here. I think I've been pushed by God. I have no other way to explain it. But Bishop Stoltzfus agreed the conversion must be spiritual, not just some ascetic desire to leave the world behind me."

He closed his eyes and pinched the bridge of his nose. "You have no idea how I've struggled since you came. I've been feeling torn between two worlds since meeting you. I'm Amish, I will stay Amish…but I also want a wife, a family." He opened his eyes and looked at her. "Now it seems *Gott* is answering my prayers. It seems my heart's desire for both is possible."

She blinked back tears. "We have a long road ahead, and it won't necessarily be a smooth one."

"Maybe not, but nothing worth having is easy. Not my magazine, not my mother's health, not your journey toward *Gott*." He took both her hands in his. "When I was younger, I thought my life would be a simple matter to plan out. But stuff happened. As much as I wanted to—or thought I could—plan my life, it has a way of surprising me with unexpected things. And those things have made me happier than I originally planned. I call that *Gott*'s will."

"To the best of my knowledge, the Bible never says 'Figure it out.'" Leah laughed shakily. "It says, 'Trust in God.' I assume God already has things figured out. If it's God's will for me to stay and be baptized, I will leave it in His hands."

"That's all I can ask for." He drew her around to face the western sky. "The long road ahead looks promising, with *Gott* at my back and you at my side. We will both leave our future in His hands."

Epilogue

L̲eah had long since left pride behind her, but she was
pleased she understood perfectly Bishop Stoltzfus's
words in *Deitsch* as she knelt before the bishop and
the deacon, in the presence of the whole community.
She placed one hand over her face, covering her eyes.
The deacon's wife removed her *kapp*, and she felt un-
clothed without it.

Speaking solemnly, the bishop intoned the ancient
words. "Are you willing, by the help and grace of *Gott*,
to renounce the world, the devil, your own flesh and
blood, and be obedient only to *Gott* and His church?"

"Yes."

"Are you willing to walk with Christ and His church
and to remain faithful through life until death?"

Leah didn't hesitate. "Yes."

"Can you confess that Jesus Christ is the Son of
Gott?"

"I confess that Jesus Christ is the Son of *Gott*."

"Can you abide by the *Ordnung* of the church according to the word of the Lord, be obedient and submissive to it, and to help therein?"

This is it, thought Leah. "I can." And immediately she felt a great weight lift off her shoulders.

"Then…" The bishop paused, and Leah heard the sound of water. She knew the deacon was pouring water into the bishop's cupped hands. "I baptize you in the name of the Father…" Water poured over her head and dripped down her neck. "And of the Son…" More water. "And of the Holy Spirit. *Amein.*"

Leah lowered her hand and smiled at the bishop, blinking through the drops running down her face. The deacon's wife handed her a clean handkerchief and waited until Leah mopped up, then—grinning—leaned down and kissed her cheek. *"Welkom,"* she murmured.

Leah laughed with pure joy. *"Danke."* She took her *kapp* from the deacon's wife and slipped it back over her hair.

The bishop helped her to her feet. "May the Lord *Gott* complete the good work which He has begun in you, and strengthen and comfort you to a blessed end through Jesus Christ. *Amein.*"

Leah felt a surge of sureness, of rightness, from the ritual. She was now a full-fledged member of the community. She turned and locked eyes with Isaac, whose face shone like a lighthouse.

This baptism had taken place on a crisp October Sabbath after the church meeting. During this service, she was the only one being baptized, unusual for the ceremony. In less than a week, she and Isaac would be wed. Edith and Ivan were to stand in lieu of parents for her during the marriage ceremony.

During the remainder of the Sabbath service, in which other ministers gave testimony about the importance of baptism, she sat next to an expectant Sarah, whose beautiful face had only grown more beautiful during her first pregnancy.

"Happy?" Sarah whispered.

"Completely," she murmured, feeling an inner glow of joy.

After the service, when people gathered to visit, Rachel bestowed a rare hug on Leah. "It's hard to believe you've been here over a year." She spoke in *Deitsch*.

"Best year of my life," replied Leah, also in *Deitsch*, nodding as Aaron joined them, standing next to Sarah, his wife.

Edith, carrying little Charity, wandered over.

"I'll take her." Leah slipped the toddler into her arms. She never lost an opportunity to hold the child, though Charity was learning to walk and more often than not wanted to practice her new skill.

"That was a lovely ceremony," said Edith. "I'm so happy for you."

"But not as happy as I am." Isaac strode up.

Leah turned to her fiancé. "Ready for the big day?" she asked, referencing their wedding that was to take place the following Thursday.

"Can't wait!" He winked.

Leah laughed, again from pure joy. The sense of love and community she had found among these people never failed to fill her cup to overflowing.

Conversation turned to general topics, but Leah found herself a bit aside, looking over the clusters of men and women and children, chattering and talking.

"Penny for your thoughts?" Isaac asked her in English, in a low voice.

"Just—just so thankful God put me here," she replied. "I mean, look at them. Every one of these people have accepted me, taught me, instructed me in the *Ordnung*, corrected me, loved me. It's something that just doesn't exist in Los Angeles." She touched her cheek, where the scar was fully healed, though still visible. Since mirrors were rare, she seldom thought about it anymore. "This is the best thing that ever happened to me. God had such plans for me, and I just couldn't see or understand them at first. But now…" She felt her eyes prickle.

"I feel the same way. When I first laid eyes on you, I knew *Gott* had sent the woman who would become my wife."

"I just didn't know about it yet."

"Oh, you knew about it right away. You just fought me tooth and nail." He grinned.

She chuckled. "It wasn't you I was fighting. It was God. Fortunately that was a battle I was happy to lose." She resisted the urge to step up and kiss him.

Kisses would come soon enough.

* * * * *

If you enjoyed this book,
be sure to check out these other titles

Seeking Refuge *by Lenora Worth*
His True Purpose *by Danica Favorite*
A Home for Her Daughter *by Jill Weatherholt*
With All Her Heart *by Kat Brookes*
A Love Redeemed *by Lisa Jordan*

Available now from Love Inspired!

Find more great reads at www.LoveInspired.com

Dear Reader,

I hope you've enjoyed my first book with Love Inspired Books. This story sprang from a deep faith as well as a lifelong love of farm life. In so many ways, the Plain People embody my world views and love of country living. For many years, I've had a deep fascination for their beliefs and lifestyle. Combine that with a long and happy marriage, and it's the perfect recipe for an Amish romance.

This story was inspired by the question of "What if?" What if a city person suddenly had her entire life stripped away and had to live in the country? Could a stranger who had never been exposed to an Amish lifestyle succeed in staying with them forever?

I love hearing from readers! Please feel free to email me at patricelewis@hotmail.com.

Blessings,
Patrice